9780901976437

THE HOUNDS OF WAR UNLEASHED

Miss Violetta Thurstan

THE HOUNDS OF WAR UNLEASHED

Violetta Thurstan

UNITED WRITERS
CORNWALL

Published by
UNITED WRITERS PUBLICATIONS
Trevail Mill - Zennor - St. Ives
Cornwall

ISBN 901976 43 1

Printed in Great Britain by
United Writers Publications
Cornwall

Dedicated to my dear friend
Kathleen Deffee,
who encouraged me to write this book.

I had met Prince Yusupov in Russia, and was delighted when he telephoned one evening saying that he was in London and that he would like to come round and see me.

He arrived a few minutes later looking very tired, but he had not lost his zest for life, and the charm which could lure a bird off a tree had not deserted him. He sat on the kitchen table dangling his legs, watching me make an omelette for our supper and talking about the Russia we both loved.

Of course there was no mention of the evil, sinister monk Rasputin. That subject was taboo, but he wanted me to tell him about the epic retreat of General Ivanov's army from the German frontier near the Masurian Lakes, back to the Ravka river – this I had experienced as I had served in Prince Volkonsky's Mobile Ambulance Unit, the Flying Ambulance.

At the beginning of the 1914-1918 war, the Russian army under Grand Duke Nicholas marched forward enthusiastically, not meeting a great deal of resistance until it crossed the German frontier and occupied Gumbinnen in Prussia. There it halted, and soon the terrible battle along the Privet marshes was joined and the reinforced pressure of the German army began to push it back until the flower of General Ivanov's army was destroyed. Back along the roads up which it had so recently marched, the remnants of the once proud Russian army retreated, slowly at first, and then with terrifying speed the German army pushed it back towards the glittering prize of Warsaw.

Our ambulances lumbered along with the army, stopping when they stopped, picking up the wounded from the hastily thrown up trenches and after bumping along the muddy Polish roads, depositing them at the nearest First Aid Post, then returning to the front once more. We seldom knew where we were going to set up our First Aid Post. Sometimes it was a country railway station, sometimes a school, and once it was a cinema in a small town, where torn pictures and broken scenery hung limply from the wall. It could be a church or a

7

village hall; once it was one of the Czar's hunting boxes in the middle of glorious forest where war should have been far away. Often the enemy was so near that we had to evacuate ourselves before we were half unpacked.

The roads to Poland were dirt roads, and when the autumn rains began they were churned up into a sort of thick porridge by the passage of heavy transport wagons, field guns and supply carts. Until the winter frosts hardened the roads, nothing but horse-drawn transport could pass, and supplies by road almost ceased. Even fodder for the horses had to be brought up the line before food and medical supplies.

The only thing plentiful was troops, thousands and hundreds of thousands of them; too many troops and not enough weapons. Unarmed soldiers had to pick up the rifles of their dead comrades and shoeless soldiers could be seen removing the field boots of the dead.

The thermometer fell far below zero when the terrible Russian winter began, when one's eyelashes crackled with ice splinters, when one was afraid to breathe deeply for fear of frozen lungs, when icicles formed into little horns in one's nostrils, melted and dripped on to one's chin, making a sore very slow to heal.

And the wounded in those days! Where they fell, there they lay until a horse-drawn cart or a sleigh could pick them up and bring them to an ambulance or a First Aid Post. The blood from their wounds would often freeze and then they would soon stiffen up and die.

Our ambulance unit had six ambulances altogether; one to travel in ourselves, and one to pick up the wounded from the field and administer first aid until they could be transferred to the base.

"You must write down all this," Prince Yusupov urged as he said goodbye, "there are so few people now who know what frightful odds there were against us, how much our soldiers suffered, and how poignant was the suffering of the people."

But I did not write the book, it was still too near. I dreamt about it at night but I did not want to talk about it.

All the time I was in Russia I used to scribble notes about the places we went to. When I had time, I wrote letters to an aunt and posted them when I could. She kept all of these, and when she died a few years ago they were returned to me in a big parcel. Nearly all were written in pencil on bits of old paper, some nearly indecipherable. But I did not want to re-read them.

Now I have gathered my courage and read and re-read the notes and letters, and hence this book. For Russia is now a closed book, divided from us by an Iron Curtain. I have seen the soul of Russia and I know how much she could have given to the world.

What has happened since the revolution is not surprising. There comes a time when suffering becomes unendurable and one must be relieved, or die. Something died in those dark days, but joy may yet come in the morning.

Before I write of what I saw in Russia, however, I must explain the why and how of that long journey.

PRELUDE

The Rally

The Rally was held in a field which slanted steeply to a sea white with heat. In the far corner, the horses were nibbling delicately at the short thyme-covered turf; overhead the gulls were swooping and wheeling, watching intently to see if there were any bits and pieces left from our picnic lunch. We F.A.N.Y.S were lolling on the grass, wishing we could bathe.

Our Training Officer came along then: "If you young things haven't signed yet, you had better go along to the Commandant's tent and do it now."

Three or four of us jumped up.

"What are we signing for?" I asked.

"You sign that you are willing to serve if there is ever a war. I think it is only a formality."

We presented ourselves, and it was only a formality. We returned to our training class.

The Training Manual said that wounded men should be wrapped warmly in blankets to lessen shock. I remembered that much later, when there were no blankets.

We were the first unit to be sent to Belgium under the auspices of St. John of Jerusalem. There were very few passengers on the boat to Ostend, only our own unit and a few young Belgians who had been called up and were on their way home. At the harbour station, the Brussels' express was drawn up in its ordinary place, but the custom house and all the usual station offices were closed. On the platform there were only two groups of harassed officials discussing the situation.

We took our seats in the train and the silence here was disconcerting and ominous. Presently the engine gave a loud screech and we crept sulkily out of the station. We did not stop anywhere on the way and were met at Brussels by a major in the khaki uniform of a British medical officer. He indicated a small van outside the station into which we fitted ourselves as best we could. In the streets we could see little groups of people looking tense and anxious, discussing their fate, but we did not see any troops.

The shops had their shutters up, and the cafe tables under the awnings were piled in an untidy heap. The van stopped at a large hotel on the main street. We were evidently expected and the head porter waiting at the front door, escorted us upstairs to the empty dining-room, bowed gravely, and left us.

Time went on and nothing happened; no one came to us. As it began to get dark, the poker-faced major who had met us at the station arrived at last and gave us the news. The German army was very near the gates. Brussels had been declared an open town and it was expected that the German troops would march in the next morning and occupy the city. There would be one more train to Ostend that night and after that there would be no more trains, out or in, and the station would be closed. He regretted very much that we should all have to go on that train and return to England. There was a gasp of dismay, and some of the party began to argue with him – but with a perfectly blank face he repeated that there was no time for discussion. The van was at the door, he added, and he would come with us to Ostend and see us on to the boat. That would be the last link with England; the steamer would not return to Ostend until Belgium had been freed. He gave us a quarter of an hour to get ready, and with heavy hearts we began to obey. As he finished, two officers, one Belgian, one English, came up to the dining-room and began an urgent discussion with him.

I watched him shake his head two or three times, then he seemed to waver and finally agreed. He called four of us out of the dining-room into an anteroom; the two medical officers came too. He told us that a very fierce battle was going on at Mons, there was great confusion and a large number of wound-ed were lying unattended. The Belgians were setting up a First Aid Post but they could not spare anyone to man it at the moment and had asked him for help. Would we four volunteer? Would we? He went on to say that there might be danger and there was no need to go unless we wished it; we could easily return with the others. Otherwise, the Belgian doctor had a car outside and was going straight to Mons himself and would take us. His car would only hold four. He must have seen from our faces that we wanted nothing better than to go. He merely added that, in that case, we must start immediately; the need was very urgent.

We had not even time to say goodbye to the others, but were hurried downstairs with the Belgian doctor. He could not speak much English, but he slapped me on the back before we got into the car and stammered, "Ladies, Belgium will always be grateful for this," and then drove off into the dark-ness. There was a continual sound of heavy guns in the distance but no traffic on the road, and the car purred along until we were suddenly ordered to stop. Lights were flashing and an obstacle was blocking the heavily guarded road.

Mary and I opened the car door as, for a long time, we had been longing desperately for a hedge and hoped to disappear into the dark night for a moment. A German officer appeared and pushed us back roughly into the car, slammed the door and, getting into the driving seat, drove off. In a few moments we stopped outside some public buildings. The Belgian doctor was ordered to produce his papers and then was hustled into the building; we never saw him again.

The officer then locked us in the car and went away. Alas, there was no hedge. We sat there in the darkness, wondering what was going to happen next. After about an hour, the Ger-man officer got into the driving seat and we entered Mons. The car stopped, the door was opened, and a voice said, "Komm," to Caroline and Anne. They followed on foot until they reached a

14

A special wartime edition postcard, produced in Paris.

Походная жизнь. Варка яицъ въ дорогѣ.

Russian soldiers on their way to the front

tall house in a side street, and Caroline and Anne were taken inside. It was now our turn. We could not see where we were going, but stumbled along a dark lane until we reached a house on a corner. Our guide thumped at the door and we were admitted.

The woman of the house looked at us with cold, hostile eyes, not uttering a word. She was obviously expecting us, for she indicated a small bedroom on the first floor containing a huge double bed which took up most of the room, and then disappeared. There was no mention of supper. I did not feel very hungry but I would have given anything for a drink; for it was a long time since we had had coffee on the steamer. There were blankets on the bed, but no pillow cases or sheets. Neither Mary nor I had ever shared a bed before but we were too tired to care, and thankfully got into our pyjamas and lay down.

Mary said in a small voice, "This 'hate' business gets me down. Why did that bitch look at us as if we were reptiles? After all, we came to help didn't we? She gives me the heeby-jeebies."

"Well, Mary, when the German officer brought us here she could see we weren't Belgian, she probably thought we were German, as we were in uniform."

Mary was horrified. "Violetta, have you realised that we are German prisoners?"

"I suppose we are. I wonder what they will do about us. There are a lot of English soldiers fighting at Mons. Wouldn't it be wonderful if they let us look after them."

"You may bet your last cent they won't do that," said Mary scornfully. "But I hope they will let us do something. We can't sit in this foul little room for ever. I'm terribly hungry, aren't you? That old toad might at least have given us a sandwich. I suppose we had better try and go to sleep and forget it."

It was hours before I could sleep; too much had happened. Only twenty-four hours ago I had been getting into the night train from Penzance to London, and here I was somewhere in Belgium, a prisoner of the Germans before I had done any of the work we had come to do. I didn't even know where Mons was on the map!

I tossed about all night, but in the morning I was in a deep sleep when a thump came on the door, and a voice from the landing said, "Frühstuck!"

"You see, they do think we are Germans," Mary. Anyway thank God there is something to eat at last."

We dressed and went downstairs. The woman we had seen the night before was there but there was no sign of her family. She evidently did not want us downstairs, for she gave us a tray with a bowl of coffee each and some bread and cheese, and motioned us to go back to our room.

I have seldom passed a more miserable day. No one came near us, so we had no news of what was going on. In the afternoon we tried to go out. We crept very quietly down the stairs but the woman appeared like a flash of lightning and held tightly to the door handle.

"Nein," she said firmly.

"Oh Lord, I wish I could speak Flemish," I said in exasperation, "I can speak German, but if I did she would only pretend she couldn't understand. I wish the doctor would come and explain."

The woman pointed to the stairs and we had to retreat. In the evening she thumped again and put a tray of food outside the door, but uttered no word. That word "Nein", in the morning was the only word we had heard since our arrival.

We discussed the situation all night, but came to no solution. We could not imagine what we had better do.

Early next morning we heard the noise of tramping feet. Tramp, tramp, tramp. We managed to open our tiny window which looked down on to the main street. We could just glimpse the opening into the town centre, and we could see what seemed to be the whole German army marching along. They were singing as they marched and appeared to be in great spirits. The tramp, tramp, tramp went on for hours until we nearly went mad.

At last, in the afternoon, there was a knock on our door and a German doctor entered. He was decidedly more agreeable than the last one and could speak a little English.

"You want to work, ladies?"

We assured him that we did. Anything to get out of the atmosphere of that horrible house.

"Then follow me, please."

German soldiers were still marching down the main street, but he led us another way until we arrived at a large building that had previously been a brewery. The ground floor which still smelt of hops, had been turned into a temporary ward; and on each iron-grey blanketed bed lay a German soldier with his bare feet sticking up.

"They have too much marched," the doctor said, "they cannot walk."

The German feet were certainly in a bad way and the soles

and even the toes of their feet, were raw and bleeding. The doctor indicated that it was our pleasant duty to put constant cold compresses on these feet, until, one presumed, they were sufficiently healed to march again against our soldiers. Personally I would have liked to put mustard plasters on them! We were left there to do as best we could; the doctor said he would send someone to fetch us in the evening.

Late that evening a young lieutenant came to escort us back to our billet. When the woman of the house opened the door for us, her face was wreathed in smiles. Evidently she had now been told that her hospitality was being given to English girls. She could not speak English and pretended she did not understand German, but she did everything she could to make us more comfortable. Sheets appeared on the bed, and a little sugar in our morning coffee. The atmosphere of hate had disappeared and we felt less depressed.

As one pair of feet resembling raw beef healed and the owner discharged, another pair belonging to another soldier who had 'too much marched' appeared to take his place. It took us the whole day making and changing the compresses and, as soon as we had finished, it was time to begin again.

Most of the soldiers were quite friendly and grateful for our ministrations and once they found that I could speak German, they chatted away quite freely. They were unable to give us much news as they knew very little about the war themselves; the only thing of which they were certain was that the war would be over by Christmas and they could go home.

During our morning walk, we noticed the reactions of the Belgians to their conquerors. In the first days of the Occupation the Germans behaved quietly and courteously - anxious to make a good impression on the inhabitants. The Belgian reaction was to ignore them and nothing they did annoyed the Germans more. If a Belgian housewife out shopping saw a German soldier in the distance, she crossed to the other side of the road to avoid him; if she met him face to face she turned to the wall and appeared to be examining it minutely. Being 'sent to Coventry' was something the Germans could not endure and a little later placards appeared on the wall, in French and Flemish, stating that if this attitude continued, the culprits would render themselves liable to punishment.

Food was getting scarce - not a real shortage, but transport of unessentials was difficult as almost all vehicles were commandeered. We passed a small German camp on our way to work each day and I saw captured Lyons tea vans and other English vehicles there. We thought it looked ominous. Meals for the patients were delivered at the brewery each day, but we had to be content with what our Belgian landlady could provide. Many mornings now, potatoes instead of bread were served for breakfast, but we did not eat much as we knew the Belgians were short of food. German soldiers were still marching through Belgium into France each day, though in smaller numbers now.

The doctor came twice a week to sign off those whose feet had recovered. He liked to practise his English and so his instructions and remarks were generally in that language and he grew more friendly as time went on. He even threw us morsels of news occasionally. There was no joy for us. The whole of Belgium was occupied and he told us that the Germans were at the gates of Paris. The doctor, too, was sure that the war would be finished before Christmas, with the Germans having won a complete and brilliant victory. He came one morning, smiling and rubbing his hands. "There is big news today."

"What news?" we asked eagerly. The absence of news from England was far worse than any other discomfort.

"There has been a naval battle and all the British fleet has been sunk."

Two of my brothers were in the navy and we had had no news of them since the war began. One was still in the Mediterranean, I hoped, but my youngest brother was in the North Sea and before we left England we had heard that his ship was still there.

I held on to the bedpost of the nearest soldier's bed. I would not show my emotion though the room was spinning dizzily around me. The doctor said something else but I could not hear what it was. Mary came to my rescue.

"Doctor, please look at the man in the corner. I think his feet are all right now." He followed her to the bed and I escaped to the little outside yard. The sun was shining; it was a dazzling day, shimmering with heat. It mocked me. It could not be that we had lost the war, that our ships were all sunk - that both my brothers were lying dead on the seabed. They were both too young to die. Oh, blast this damned war! I wished - no - it wasn't any goodwishing. Perhaps they were prisoners; that would be something, but not much. Mary and I were getting it very easy but prison camp for them would be a different thing.

Mary joined me in the yard. "He's gone - damn him. Don't believe it for a moment, Violetta; he only said that to torment you."

The woman at our billet was very friendly now and I asked

18

her that evening if she had heard any news of our navy. She replied that the Germans had forbidden publication of any Belgian paper under pain of severe punishment. She had heard rumours of a battle in the North Sea, but she did not know if it were true, so there was nothing to do but wait and hope. I must never give up hope.

Three weeks passed and there was never any news. We had very few patients as most of them had recovered and gone back to the front. The doctor came in one morning with a sheaf of instructions in his hand.

"We are closing this place down, ladies; there is nothing for you to do here."

I was glad; I did not want to see any more feet.

"What are you going to do with us?" Mary said.

"You will return to Brussels tomorrow."

"Brussels! Tomorrow? What shall we do there?"

"You will see. Maybe they will send you back to England."

"Pigs might fly," said Mary, "but I don't think they will."

The doctor looked furious. I think he thought we were calling him a pig. He turned his back and left the room. I was sorry if we had hurt his feelings because he had been reasonably friendly to us. If it had been the lieutenant I suppose we should have been shot at dawn.

Next morning, the unamiable lieutenant knocked at the door and told us to bring our things and come downstairs. An ambulance was outside; the lieutenant motioned us to get in, and after slamming the door, he got up beside the driver. There was no sign of Caroline and Anne.

It was a long and dismal drive, for the dark blinds were pulled down in the ambulance so that we could see nothing. After driving for what seemed months, the ambulance stopped and we decanted ourselves in front of a large house with the title "Institut des Jeunes Filles' over the door. A soldier was standing against the railing. We were directed to a little empty office; presently a severe-looking German woman entered, holding some keys.

"You will sleep in No. 43," she said to me and, turning to Mary, "here is a key for you, No. 62 on the floor above. My office is in the hall and is open from nine to eleven each morning. You will not leave the house without permission from me and you will keep the rules of the house. Your lights will be out by nine-thirty each evening. Now you will have your supper. You will find some of your compatriots in the dining-room. Berthe will show you to your room," she added as she left the room.

A down-trodden looking Belgian maid preceded us up the stairs. I was dreadfully disappointed to be separated from Mary, but the warden looked impervious to any argument.

There were three beds in room 43, but the other occupants were not there. I did not want any supper but I urgently wanted to see Mary, so I went downstairs. The enormous salle-à-manger was just in front of me when I opened the door. There must have been more than one hundred and fifty women of all ages there. Most of them looked English. I noticed that every-one had a disc with the number of their room beside them, so I went round looking for No. 43, keeping my eyes open for Mary. No one took any notice of me but at last I came to an empty place, and thankfully saw a disc marked 43 beside it. I sat down and looked at my companions. One was a French girl who was looking up words in a dictionary; the other was English. The English girl looked up from her plate.

"Have you just come?" she asked.

"Yes, my friend and I have just arrived."

"Well, as you can see, you have come to a mad-house."

"Who are all these people?" I asked.

"The Germans had the splendid idea of rounding up all the English in Brussels - nannies, governesses, maids, office girls, nurses, Uncle Tom Cobbly and all, and packed them in here. There is nothing whatever to do, and we all quarrel and grumble all day."

"What are they going to do with us?"

"The Lord above only knows, my dear. In the mean time, as you are going to sleep in our room, you might tell me your name and what brought you here."

I told her as much as I thought was good for her while I looked around for Mary. I could not see her so I went to bed hating this place and everyone in it.

One might have been at school again. In the morning a clanging bell sounded in the corridor, and a harsh voice called, "Aufstehen, aufstehen." My companions did not stir, but I got up and crept down quickly. The first people I saw in the dining-room were Anne and Caroline, who beckoned to me to come and sit beside them. They had heard all our news from Mary as she had been allotted to their room. We had passed the house where they had been billeted every day on our way to the brewery, but had never caught a glimpse of them.

"We weren't there," related Caroline, "they sent us back to Brussels the day after you and Mary left us, and we have been here ever since. At first there were only a few of us, but more and more people arrived every day, till now there isn't room for a sardine. There is a rumour that we shall be sent back to England, but how could we? We can't swim. I wish every day of my life that we had never volunteered to go to Mons. There are no letters, no newspapers, no news from home in this squalid place. If it hadn't been for Anne I should have been dotty long ago."

Anne also had comments, "The first people were all supposed to be English, but there are a lot of different nationalities now and I know some of them are informers who report everything we say. We have to be jolly careful who we talk to - it isn't safe to talk to anybody. This place was a girls' school before the war - all evacuated now of course. There's a chapel in the grounds and Caroline and I slip in after supper most nights to discuss things. They put the lights out at nine-thirty sharp but we generally have time first to discuss plans. You and Mary must come with us tonight."

Mary came to breakfast at this point.

"Violetta, you know that woman said last night we mustn't go out without her permission. It is Sunday tomorrow; shall we ask for a pass to go to Mass? There's a church just across the road."

That seemed a very good idea. We were both Catholics, and anyway we were longing to get out alone. We got our passes easily, allowing us out for an hour, and we had to show them to the sentry at the door.

It was a large, unfashionable church and was crowded to the door but we found two empty seats.

We had got as far as the Creed when there was a great commotion at the door. A white-faced boy, who looked about fourteen, rushed into the church holding some newspapers tight to his chest. He looked round wildly and finally fled into a Confessional and lay on the floor.

The next moment three German soldiers tramped into the church, stopped Mass, and began to search the whole place. There was dead silence as the soldiers went from pew to pew looking for the boy. At last they approached the Confessional where he was hiding. A sigh went up from the congregation as one of the soldiers triumphantly pulled him out by his shoulders and we saw him, still with his papers, being dragged out of the church door, sobbing and imploring mercy. Most of the congregation were sobbing too as it was brought home so visibly what this military occupation was going to mean for them. After about ten minutes wait, the priest finished the Mass and we returned to the Institut. The boy had been delivering 'Le Courier de Bruxelles', a tiny clandestine paper much in favour in Brussels, but fraught with great danger for those who produced and distributed it. Death was the normal penalty.

Mary and I were completely shattered by this incident and wished we could avoid our rendezvous with Caroline and Anne. But Caroline whispered to me as we were about to enter the dining-room that there was some good news for us. So later we made our way to the garden and found the chapel open. It was dark inside, though it was still bright outside, and just one single red light glimmered in front of the altar. Caroline told us that she and Anne were planning to get a pass, to put on their oldest clothes, wearing the Red Cross brassards that had been supplied when we first came out to Belgium, and go on foot to the gates of Brussels. These were heavily guarded and theoretically no one could get through without a pass. Actually there were country carts with produce for Brussels constantly passing through, and when the guards saw the same carts going back empty, they generally waved them on. Caroline's plan was to follow one of the carts out. The man, or sometimes an old woman, always walked through leading their horses, and these two would follow behind as if they belonged to the family.

Mary was horrified at this plan. She was easily the most practical of us all.

"But how do you know all this, my dear?"

"Berthe! Berthe! Berthe!" Caroline replied triumphantly. "Her family have a horse and cart and bring vegetables in every day."

"Berthe! She looks much too stupid to be any good, "Mary said. "She might easily give you away without meaning to. You said yourself there were some funny sorts of people in this house who would get a very good reward for denouncing you."

"Not at all. Berthe is not nearly so stupid as she looks. She would dearly love to cock a snook at the Boche if she got a chance."

"And having got out, what would you do then? Would you swim across the Channel? This part of Belgium is Flemish speaking. Do either of you speak Flemish? You will only get caught and put in prison. This place is grim, but a German prison will be a lot grimmer."

"We both thought you would be thrilled at being in on this, but since you aren't interested, don't bother. Anyhow, it would be much more difficult for four people than for two. Let's say no more. I for one am going to bed."

Mary was worried at having upset Caroline. After all, we were all F.A.N.Y.s and perhaps it was our duty to try and escape. But she still thought the whole plan was quite mad. As she shared a room with Anne and Caroline, she could not help knowing that they were going on quietly with their plans without saying anything to her.

Then something happened that shook us. It was towards the end of October when we were all summoned to the dining-room, whether to hear good news or bad we did not know. A German officer stood at the head of the table with some papers in his hand. The Directrice of the Institut stood beside him. He signalled for silence.

"Ladies, I have to announce to you that you will be leaving by train on Wednesday. You will be ready at twelve noon with your things packed. Transport will be provided to take you to

23

the station."

He left the room without mentioning our destination. That gave us two days before we left Brussels, and the dining-room buzzed with conjecture. We were going to England – no, we should all be interned in Berlin; no, someone had informed the Germans of the indiscreet things we sometimes said, and we should be put in prison. Caroline and Anne were sure that Berthe had reported our conversation to the warden and rushed upstairs to interrogate her, but she was not cleaning the bed-rooms as usual, in fact we never saw her again.

On Wednesday we were down to breakfast very early, our things packed and ready. The Directrice was sitting in her place and rose when we had all assembled. She announced a change in the arrangements. The journey had been postponed; we should now travel on the following Sunday.

The early excitement had died away. I think most of us were apprehensive as to what the future would bring. The days until Sunday seemed very long. No more passes were allowed, and Anne and Caroline were more than ever sure that their plans had been discovered.

On Sunday morning the Directrice rose once more to make an announcement. Our journey had been postponed again. We were all very jittery by this time and most felt that this second postponement meant nothing good for us. There was a new rumour every day. One of the party who had been house-keeper at the American Ambassador's private residence in Brussels, had heard that he was trying to get us exchanged for some German sailors whose ship had been blown up by our navy, and that the longer we were kept here the better, as it showed that he was probably negotiating our release with some success.

The next announcement was at supper on the following Tuesday. We were told for the third time to be packed and ready the next morning. And this time it really happened.

About noon, several big buses drew up at the front door and we knew we were really going – "Where?" – we asked the Directrice. "I do not know; you will see," she replied indif-ferently.

Part of the Brussels station had been cleared for our large party of about one hundred and fifty English women. Three or four soldiers stood round us trying to keep the onlookers away – with small success. They crowded round us, asking where we were going, and giving the names of friends in England to whom they wanted to send messages. They got tired after a while, the soldiers kept telling them to go away, and we had been standing there more than an hour.

The crowd had thinned, but there were still a number of people waiting to see what was going to happen. I felt a tug at my skirt and I looked around.

"Hush," whispered a voice. "Don't look at me, I want to ask you a great favour."

"What is it?" I whispered back.

She produced a letter, hiding it in her dark coat so that I could only see a corner of it. "I have not had any news of my husband since the Boche arrived. I have no money. He must help me. I have written to him and I ask you to take the letter."

"I am so sorry, I cannot do that – I should be caught. They are sure to search us."

"Where are you going?"

"We don't know – nobody knows. But I know we daren't carry letters. "I looked round to see if any of the soldiers were watching us, but they too were getting bored with the long wait and were chatting together.

"You are English, yes? I am Belgian but my husband is English and he has gone off and left me here alone and I have no money. I shall starve," she said, beginning to cry. I wavered, it seemed awful not to help this poor woman.

"Where is your husband?"

"He is in St. Petersburg. He is a teacher of languages there."

"Russia is the last place I am ever likely to go to," I muttered.

"Talking is forbidden!" shouted one of the soldiers.

The woman instantly melted into the crowd and I was left with the envelope which had been pushed into my hand. I felt very uneasy and did not know what to do with it. I quite expected to be shot then and there if the soldiers caught sight of it. I hastily put it under my left armpit. Mary was standing next to me and had heard most of the conversation.

"Blow me down if that woman hasn't got a nerve," she muttered as she came nearer and pressed up against my left shoulder. "Stick close to me, and perhaps you can stoop down and put it into the top of your stocking."I tried, it was difficult to get it in, but I managed to put it under the elastic of my knickers. I thought it would be safe there for the present, I still felt terribly worried about this letter and looked around again to see if I could see anything of this woman, but she had melted into the crowd.

We were dreadfully tired after standing so long, but there was nowhere to sit and the soldiers wouldnot allow us to move

25

out of the close circle we made in the middle of the platform. I began to feel that I could not bear it a moment longer when, very slowly, a long black train came writhing into the station and stopped at our platform.

The soldiers marshalled us towards the train. A lieutenant had taken his place there beside the open door of one of the compartments and as that filled up he moved to the next one. Soon we were all in the train, the outer doors were locked, and the blinds pulled down. Seven of us were allotted to each carriage and a soldier was camped in the corner of each compartment. It was another hour and a half before the train moved majestically out of the station. The soldiers had probably had a meal and we had not. We were extremely hungry and wondered when the next meal was coming.

The soldier in our carriage seemed to be a deaf mute, he neither looked at us, nor spoke. The train went on, and on, and on. No food appeared. We had no idea where we were going. Someone suggested that we were going to Holland to be interned but most people thought we were going to Berlin.

Late that night we got to a big station and waited there a very long time. I was in the corner opposite the soldier. He appeared to be dozing, so I pulled the blind aside a very little way and tried to read the name on the platform lamp. It was Liège. I knew this was the frontier station for Germany. I told Mary, who had managed to get a seat next to me.

"Berlin is to be our destination, I suppose," was her only comment. The soldier began to wake up so I dropped the blind. It was a hot night for the beginning of November and we were terribly thirsty. I asked the soldier if we could have something to drink. He did not answer, but he called another soldier to come and stand at our door while he went away. He came back with a bucket of clear, cold water and a mug. So he was not a deaf mute after all, and we were very grateful.

We tried to sleep, but it was a horrible train; it rocked and bumped, and every time I was nearly asleep it jerked me awake again. The Germans had not put on their best railway stock for us; the seats were of the straight-up hard wooden variety, made, I suppose, in the first days of railway transport.

In the morning we arrived at an important station; I think it was Cologne. It certainly was in Germany, and there were several German officers awaiting our train. Here we changed guards. The blinds were pulled up and the windows opened to allow a cup of coffee and a biscuit each to enter the carriage. An old woman with a broom appeared and swept out the debris from each carriage. After this, we felt nearly human again. The worst snag was that there was no water in the wash place; it had been used up the day before and they did not renew it. The officer in charge of the train came through and counted us. The new guard with a rifle attached like the last one, got into his corner, the blinds were pulled down again, the door slammed, and we were off once more on this mysterious journey.

All day we went further and further into Germany. In the early evening we got to a station named Munster. Our guard instructed us to get out and follow the train commandant along the platform. No passengers were allowed on the platform but a large number of German civilians were clustered outside a waiting room and they hissed at us, and shouted curses at the damn English, one or two spat at us. We were ushered into a long dark room under the station. Here a sort of supper was set and German Red Cross sisters served us with tea, sandwiches and cheese. They evidently found their task very distasteful for their faces were grim and they did not speak to us. I spoke to one of them who looked more forthcoming than the others and asked her if she knew where we were going.

"I do not know," she replied, "we had orders to get a meal for some English women going to Berlin, so I suppose you will go there presently." The woman in charge looked furious when she saw her assistant speaking to us, and she immediately sent her off to another part of the room.

We stayed in this room all night. It had a lavatory attached, so we were able to wash ourselves a little in turns, and were thankful to be out of the rattling train.

Early in the morning some coffee arrived, the train commandant opened the door, and we were led upstairs on to a platform where a train was standing. There were no people about this time, we were thankful to see.

The third soldier we had had as guard since we started was the best of the lot. He would not tell us where we were going, perhaps he did not know, but he did tell us in the evening that a big station where we had stopped for some hours was Hamburg, which was his home town. But that was not the way to Berlin. Where were they going to send us? I began to get anxious for Mary; she looked so exhausted that I did not think she would stand much more of this.

In the afternoon the soldier allowed us to pull up the blinds. We were going along through a very flat country with a lot of green fields and hundreds of cows; there did not seem to be any inhabitants. Late in the afternoon we stopped as usual for a very long time, and then the train commandant came along and opened the carriage door.

"Ladies," he said, "your journey is ended; this is Denmark." We could not believe it at first. We got slowly out of the train. There were a lot of people on another platform, waving and smiling at us. We walked across the frontier, and we were free. Free in Denmark!

A train was drawn up marked 'Copenhagen' and we were told to get in although we had no tickets and no money. As soon as we were on the train the Red Cross sisters and other people came round bringing flowers, sweets, chocolates, magazines, sandwiches and coffee – hugging us and telling us how glad they were that we were safe. They had been told in the morning that we were on our way and had prepared this wonderful, wonderful welcome. We were quite overcome by it. Mary collapsed altogether and was led off by a sympathetic Danish sister.

I had an idea. My Aunt Evie's greatest friends were the St.Johns at the Legation in Copenhagen. If one of the sisters would telephone to the Legation for me, they would send a message home to say I was safe. One came along with a cup of coffee. I asked her if this could be managed and she hurried off at once to do it.

These kind people arranged to take over a wing of an hotel in Copenhagen to house our large party; we were to stay there till London could arrange and send instructions for our journey home.

A sister had taken charge of Mary and she came back soon and said it had been arranged for her to go to a nursing home for a rest. She did not want me to visit her until she was better. I was dreadfully worried, I thought she must be really ill, and no wonder.

When we arrived at the station in Copenhagen, there was someone to meet me from the Legation and to take me off to the St.Johns' for a few days. I shall never forget their kindness and the affectionate welcome. They made me go to bed at once and said they would hear my story next day. They had already sent a telegram home to say I was staying with them.

No one could have been kinder to me than the St.Johns. I had no money but they provided as much as I needed; I had no clothes, but Mrs St.John took me out shopping and I bought a new outfit. She knew I was worried about Mary and took me one afternoon to see her. I found her better but not allowed to get up yet.

There was another kindness the next day which the St. Johns' arranged - a very small dinner party to celebrate my escape. Their old friend Prince Gustav of Denmark was anxious to hear our story and arranged for me to sit next to him at dinner. We got along very well together and he was very much interested in our doings and asked a thousand questions. He called at their house again the following day and said he was going to drive out to the fortifications, and asked if I would like to come too.

Prince Gustav was driving himself and I sat on the front seat with him; his chauffeur sat at the back. After the horrible months I had endured, it was heaven to be driving out into the country on this sunny blue day. We went round the fortifications together and although I was very ignorant of such things, I could not help thinking that they looked rather inadequate. I had seen the might of the German army marching out of the gates at Mons. I had seen the cowed people in Brussels suffering indignities of every kind. I could not help wondering if little Denmark would ever suffer the same fate as little Belgium.

We had lunch between two sheltering rocks, looking down on the peaceful pastoral scene and I was miles away when Prince Gustav suddenly said, "I had a letter from my aunt this morning, the Dowager Empress of Russia, and she told me that they are having a devastating time in Russia. They were not prepared for such a number of wounded, supplies are very short and she is very much distressed and anxious. There are hundreds of thousands of soldiers available in Russia but at the front, though they are not short of man power, they are dreadfully short of equipment and supplies.

"Would you like to go to Russia and help?"

I was stunned and could not answer for a long time. At last I said, "Yes, indeed, I should love to go and help - I would go tomorrow if I could. But you see, I have to go wherever I am sent. I don't know if our H.Q. in London would let me."

When I thanked him for the lovely drive he said, "I am sending a courier tonight to my aunt. May I say you would like to go?"

"Yes, indeed," I answered, "only do say that I cannot go unless I am ordered by the St. Johns' people."

"I think that will be all right," he said, smiling, "my aunt is a very determined woman."

And by the narrowest shave, with twelve hours to spare, 'the determined woman' got her way.

30

A communication to the minister arrived in the Chancery in the first Diplomatic Bag from London. It asked that the Minister to Denmark would be good enough to arrange the departure of our very large party to England as soon as practicable. There was no word from Russia. I was not exactly disappointed, I should have been happy to go there and do my utmost to help, but I also had a letter in the bag which made me very homesick. It was from Aunt Evie, saying how wonderful it was to hear that I was safe and could be home soon, and that she was counting the minutes until she saw me again. She gave me news of my brothers, they were both safe. My younger brother had been in a battle in the North Sea but no particulars had come through as yet.

Then came orders from the Minister. Arrangements were being made for us all to return to England. We might have to go at very short notice indeed and were to keep ourselves in readiness to depart directly the necessary instructions came through. We said goodbye with many thanks to our kind friends in Denmark. We packed. We jumped every time the telephone rang and at last were told that transport would be sent to fetch us the following morning. The telephone rang again just as we were going up to bed and this time it was a personal message for me. The permission to go to Russia and put myself at the disposal of the Empress had just come through.

We were all at the hotel now. I had transferred myself directly I heard the news of our departure. Mary had left the nursing home that afternoon to be with us when the call came. She was bitterly disappointed that I was not going home with her after all we had been through together. She wished I had asked Prince Gustav to let her come to Russia with me. I wished it too - it would have been a great adventure for us to start off together, but she was not at all fit yet; she was very white and shaky, and I think she realised herself that the adventure was not for her.

The call for the party going to England came just after breakfast. I watched them all go, but I was not allowed to see them off. None of them knew how they were going but, unlike the last journey, they knew where they were going. Home.

I had a few qualms when they were all gone, but the kind and generous St.Johns said I must return to the Legation until everything was fixed for my journey. When she rang up, Mrs St.John told me that Prince Gustav was coming that evening and that he would give me all the details. She added that he was very much pleased that I had had permission to go.

For several days I waited impatiently for the official permission authorising me to start out on my long Russian journey. Late one night a thick envelope full of passes and instructions arrived at the Legation, and by the next evening my new found Danish friends, with their hands full of gifts, chocolate, magazines and flowers, were gathering at Copenhagen station to see me off to Russia.

The first lap of the journey was very easy. The Copenhagen to Stockholm International train rolled itself on to the night ferry which crossed the narrow channel to the Swedish port of Malmö, the southernmost tip of Sweden. Berths were made up while people went into the restaurant, and presently the train rolled itself up the ramp on to the railway line leading to Stockholm.

We arrived in Stockholm early in the morning, but not early enough for the Lapland Express which I missed by ten minutes. As there was only one train a day I made for the nearest hotel to wait until morning. I was received at the reception desk by a pretty fair-haired girl, full of smiles. Yes, there was a vacant room and perhaps I would like to go to the dining-room for some coffee while it was being got ready. A waiter brought some coffee and asked for my passport which he took away with him.

I dallied over my delicious Swedish breakfast until I thought my room would be ready. I then went to the reception desk where the atmosphere had completely changed.

"Is my room ready now?" I asked.

"There is no room," was the sullen reply.

"But you said there was a room. You said it would be ready very soon."

The girl looked supremely uncomfortable and coloured up. "There is no room," she said, "there was a mistake." She handed me my passport.

I could not imagine what had happened. I would not ask any more questions, but I felt very worried. I picked up my two cases and prepared to go. An old gentleman got out of his chair in the lounge and nudged my arm, "They won't have you because they are very pro-German," he whispered. "Try the hotel opposite; you will be all right there."

Then I realised what had happened. At the reception desk there was a notice, 'German Spoken', and as I did not know any Swedish, I had asked in German if I could have a room. I thanked the old gentleman and left the hotel immediately.

I was so furious at this reception that I nearly decided to stay at the station all night. On reflection I thought it would hurt no one but myself. I had better try the other hotel first. They were so charming and welcoming there that I blurted out my whole story.

"Oh that hotel," they said laughing, "those German people, they almost want to see your pedigree before you get a room. I expect they thought you were German until they saw your passport. Never mind, you will be all right now," and so I was, but I was afraid to go out, and I stayed in the hotel all day. They loaded me with food and kindness, escorted me over to the station next morning, and provided me with a bag of sandwiches and cakes for the journey.

It was very exciting to travel in a train labelled 'Lapland Express'. I wished Mary had been with me; she would have loved it as much as I did. All day the train travelled up the coast. Its final destination was the big iron ore place, Narvik, far north of the Arctic Circle, but I had to change later that night at Boden and travel by sleigh to the Russian frontier as there was no rail communication at that time between Sweden and Russian Finland.

The train was pretty full when we started that morning with our noses pointing towards the North Pole, but as the black winter afternoon turned into night the passengers began getting out at every stop. No one got in, and the train was almost empty when we got to Haparanda. We climbed down reluctantly from the warm fuggy carriage on to the squeaking, down-trodden snow covering the platform. There were only five passengers left beside myself. A Finnish farmer, a Swedish-American agent for something or other, his chère amie, and Elsa, a Finnish Red Cross nurse who, as I found out afterwards, had been training for a year or two in a London hospital. And, of course, an 'experienced traveller' - most journeys have one.

Several sleighs harnessed to restless stamping ponies were drawn up round the station. I wondered what I was supposed to do next.

C

"Come along with me," suggested the experienced traveller, instantly selecting the best of the vehicles. "You look a sensible girl and travel light," he added, looking disapprovingly at the mountain of luggage the chère amie was collecting round herself.

"Too light," I murmured, shivering.

His own collection of well bred luggage was not inconsiderable, so it was a good thing that I hadn't much. I got in and cowered in the hay; the experienced traveller was behind me. The Lapp driver climbed into his seat and made chuckling noises at the ponies, the bells jingled and, with a lurch forward we were off into the night. It was marvellous. The ponies went full gallop in the starlight over the frozen snow of the track, the air was like wine, and I would not have changed places with a king. For a time!

Presently the cold began to penetrate, my breath froze and it hurt to swallow. My eyes were rimmed with prickling ice, and no huddling into the hay on the floor of the sleigh would alleviate that sinister frightening cold. I thought of home, 'Cornish Riviera'. What a mockery that word was. I thought of the great log fires, with the thick sheepskin rug in front of the hearth in the drawing-room, and my teeth chattered like castanets.

I wondered why I had come . . . Would you go home if you could, you coward? You know you wouldn't. There is an immeasurable gulf between those who are in the war and those who are outside it. You wouldn't like to be outside it? You wouldn't – well then. But all the same, I wish I wasn't so terribly cold. Try and remember what it was like to be hot. Do you remember the Rally, how we all lay on the grass and panted like dogs? And that time coming back from Milan, when it was too hot to bear even a newspaper on your knee? Did I really grumble about the heat? I couldn't have . . .

I was asleep when sometime that night a faceless figure lifted me out of the sleigh. We had stopped at an inn, a primitive wooden affair, and we were going to spend the rest of the night there. It was gloriously hot inside and the burning birchwood logs filled the room with fragrance. I felt giddy and sat down on the nearest chair.

"You'd better have some of this, little English girl."

I looked round in a daze. It was Persson, the American Agent who was leaning over his lady friend with a steaming glass.

"What is it?"

34

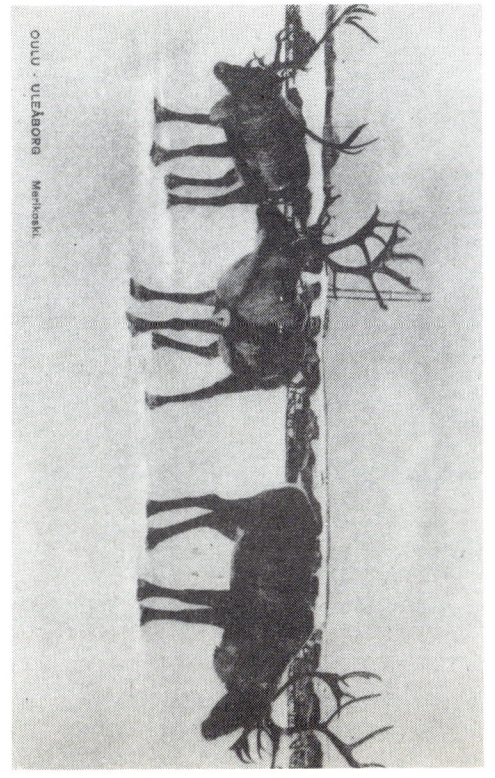

OULU · ULEÅBORG   Merikoski

Lapland

Lapland

"Swedish punch, honey, I guess it's the finest drink God ever made to keep out the cold. It's forty below here."

Elsa, the Red Cross nurse, was already sipping primly from a glass; the others were all smoking, drinking and laughing. I felt humiliated. They were all tougher than me. But I was tough too, they would see.

The host was already beside me with a steaming glass, and I tasted the contents. My godfathers, they were right. It was so potent that my whole being seemed to be on fire, and my throat seared with hot iron. In a few minutes the glow had spread to my fingers and the room seemed to get larger and the people in it appeared to be giants.

"I think I had better go to bed," I said to the room.

They all laughed, and my host's wife patted me on the back, lit a candle and led me off to bed.

"Good night, little English girl," they shouted after me, preparing for a merry night downstairs.

Hours after that Elsa came up to bed. I opened my eyes.

"I thought I had better wake you," she said, "look at the sky."

I emerged from the mound of bedclothes and looked at a brilliant incandescent sky with darting, leaping flames.

"They're the Northern Lights. We have them in Finland too, of course, but not as good as this. Persson says they are brighter here than anywhere else in the world. But of course we are very far north here you know. We are near the Arctic Circle. I thought you would like to see them. I know you don't have them in England."

I should have liked to watch these celestial fireworks all night but it was not possible to keep my eyes open. I shall never forget, though, that first night in Lapland.

We got up in the frosty dawn. This was to be an exciting day - the Russian frontier this afternoon. A group of Lapps were waiting outside the inn with sleighs drawn by reindeer. They were incredibly dirty, but joyously gay with flamboyant fur boots turned up at the toes and red feathers in their stocking caps.

We drove for an eternity through a forlorn land. First of all it was all bog and snow drift, with an occasional granite boulder clothed with greenish-white lichen to diversify the landscape. Later came a dark forest, full of Christmas trees thick with snow, and gnarled stunted birches concealing gnomes and piskies in their rimed branches. We had stepped off the end of the world and a most uncanny and frightening place lay before us.

In the early afternoon, just as the blood-red sun was setting over the ice, we drove over a great frozen river towards a collection of red-painted wooden buildings. This was Tornea.

Russia lay beyond.

Crossing the frontier into Russia is not a light-hearted matter of showing a passport and perfunctorily opening a suit-case or two. A sentry with an open bayonet shepherded our little group to a door in the building and motioned us in. The others obeyed instantly, but when I saw my luggage being taken off in the opposite direction I protested vigorously.

The Experienced Traveller pushed me towards the door. "Come along, don't be a little fool. You had much better do as you are told if you want to get into Russia." I followed him but with many misgivings. We entered a large hall with wooden benches all round it and a lot of people sitting there. One would have expected it to be noisy, with gossip and laughter, but it was a strangely silent crowd.

A soldier collected all our passports and papers and went away, the door clanging after him in a sort of determined way.

Hour after hour passed and nothing happened. I began to get into a panic. One feels very defenceless in a strange country without passport or luggage, or even a language to communicate one's fears. What had gone wrong? I had come all this way – and now they wouldn't let me in. How could I get home again if they turned me away? I was not the only one panicking. There was a young man with a girl of about my own age, walking up and down the hall, both of them crying bitterly and kissing each other passionately. Neither of them took the slightest notice of any of us, and no one tried to help them. The sentry at the door looked formidable and disapproving.

At last another soldier came to the door and bawled out a name. Elsa, the nurse from Finland, got up and followed him and then there was a long pause.

The soldier reappeared at last and shouted out a name. Nobody moved. He called again and I saw them all looking at me. A third time, and this time I distinguished Violetta some-thing. So I got up and followed him out.

We went along a passage to a small office where three men

37

were sitting, one in plain clothes, the other two in uniform. My papers were spread out before them. The man in plain clothes began to speak in correct but very stiff English.

"Well, Mademoiselle, why do you want to come to Russia?"

"I am going to serve in your Red Cross," I answered. "I am going to the front."

"Have you ever been to Russia before? Do you know anyone here?"

"No, I don't know anybody. I have never been to Russia."

"Why then do you wish to nurse our wounded. Are there no English wounded that you can help?"

I had never pictured this kind of reception. I thought once I got to Russia I should be received with open arms, but I did not seem to be wanted. I made a great effort.

"They told me about the thousands and thousands of wounded in Russia. In England we have so many people to help, and so many hospitals and comforts for the wounded. I wanted to help the ones who have so few comforts. And," I added lamely, "I am very strong and healthy and I don't mind hard work or hardships."

I looked down at his desk and saw my passport on it. Underneath it was a paper with a Red Cross heading, so I knew that they were expecting me, and were only trying me out. Though why, I could not imagine.

"You are very welcome, Mademoiselle. There are many wounded and much suffering. Who knows how it will all end?" He sighed profoundly and tugged at his ample moustache.

"Here are your papers. Do not trouble about your luggage, the porter will put it in the train. I wish you a happy journey."

That had been an alarming beginning. I was still sweating with apprehension when I followed the soldier to the platform where a great train was steaming in the frozen air. He put my things on a seat and pointed to a buffet where I found Elsa, the Finnish nurse, radiant at having got through customs formalities. She beckoned me to come and sit beside her.

"You must let me give you supper, I had so many nice suppers in England. Now I am finished with papers, I must wait until my father comes to fetch me; he has a timber business here."

I was ravenous after all this agitation and thankful to see food. A broad-beamed woman in a wadded coat served us with little fish piès, pickled mushrooms and a hard boiled egg. The samovar bubbled merrily, providing glasses of sweet weak tea for the people who began crowding in now.

In the corner of the restaurant was an ikon with a large red lamp burning before a representation of Our Blessed Lady and the Child. Few of the crowd scrambling for food took any notice of it, but I was rather shocked to see a stout young man crossing himself devoutly with his lighted cigarette. I suppose he was murmuring prayers of gratitude at having survived the ordeal of the customs' examination.

The couple who were so tearful and agitated did not re-appear. I felt very unhappy for them and hoped that whatever happened to them, at least they would be together.

A deep clanging bell boomed once, twice, three times, for the train to start and, at last, late in the night, we slowly pulled out. I felt very glad to be in Russia at last.

When I unpacked a few things for the night, I found my suitcase had been disarranged, so they had searched my luggage after all.

Before I took my seat, I went out on to the swaying plat-form that divided the coaches to look at Finland. The moon had risen, and the full moon and the lighted train between them threw deep shadows on the forests of pines bending under the weight of frosted snow, and now and then we passed glades of silver birches which seemed to be dancing like beautiful ladies in the moonlight. Three white colours, all different, the pearl white of the moon, the silver white of the birches, the opaque white of the snow. A curious theatrical effect.

It was too cold to stay more than a few minutes, and I had to return to my carriage. It had filled up since I left and we all settled down for the night, tightly bunched together in a tropical climate. There was a stove in each section of the train and the old man who looked after it had filled it up with wood until it was red hot. Then, I suppose, he retired to his slum-bers, for in the morning it was so cold that the windows were covered with frost crystals and we could not see out. Every-one was cursing the old boy for letting out the stove and he appeared to be very humiliated and apologetic.

How much I wished I could speak Russian. How right Prince Gustav was when he had said laughingly that I ought to learn Russian before going off to nurse Russian soldiers.

The Finnish landscape was unchanged as we went on all day. We loitered through interminable forests, so lonely and desolate they looked. Our pace was slow because the fuel for the engine was wood and we had to stop frequently to fill up the tender. Here and there was a clearing with great piles of logs beside a little station, with a few red and white cottages surrounding it. Then we made a stop, sometimes a long one,

39

where there was a buffet and we could get out of the train and go and buy food, slices of dried reindeer meat, pickled herrings, and occasionally some black or yellow caviare. There are some who like it. I am not one of these. I have my greeds, but addiction to caviare is not one of these; it is sougly.

It was after one of these stops that a girl wearing a Red Cross brassard squeezed her way into our carriage. Some-one at the last stop had told her that there was an English girl on the train who could not understand any Russian, and she had come along to see if she could help. Her name was Marie Ivanova, she told me, and she had been to school in Folkestone for five years and was on her way now to Petrograd. She hoped to be accepted for war work in one of the medical units. Marie was very pretty and charming; she spoke English as well as I did and we clicked at once. I told her I was feeling nervous about our arrival in Petrograd, as I did not know what I was expected to do, or where to go.

"Oh, you must come with me," she said, "there's sure to be someone meeting me at the station. Anyway, I want to stay a night or two at the hotel and get tidied up before I face my relations there."

That was exactly what I wanted most; I had never felt so dirty in my life. The train was filthy and the lavatories were always full of sleeping soldiers. Anyway, there was no water in them, and except for sponging my face at some of the stations, I had not been able to wash properly since leaving Stockholm.

We arrived at last in the dark and dirty Finland station at Petrograd, and Marie and I were thankful when a Red Cross official of some kind met us when we got out of the train, say-ing that rooms had been reserved for us both at the Hotel Angleterre. He packed us into a sleigh and separated.

Marie pointed out several landmarks as we went along but I was too tired and dirty to get any impression of Petrograd at all.

The room that Marie and I shared in the hotel was warm, the bath water was hot and I could not wait to get into it. As I threw off my dirty clothes I found in the hem of my coat the letter that the Belgian woman had given me at the Brussels station. I had folded it up small and had managed to hide it in what I felt sure was a very safe place and then had forgotten all about it. How little I had thought then that I would ever be in Russia.

The envelope had a Petrograd address on it and I thought I would try to find this husband of hers somewhere and give myself the pleasure of telling him I had seen his wife, and that she had given me this letter which I had carried all the way from Brussels.

Then I leapt into the bath for which I had been longing for such ages, and was wallowing in it when there was a loud knock on the door. Marie opened it and shouted to me to hurry up as there was a General somebody waiting downstairs to see us. I flew into my clothes and we ran down into the hall where an enormous and most impressive general, covered with stars and medals, was waiting. I may have been dishevelled, but how glad I was that I was clean.

He brought exciting news. Her Majesty, the Dowager Empress, would like to see the two Red Cross nurses, and a car would arrive the next afternoon to take us to the Palace. He would give himself the pleasure of accompanying us there. What a wonderful way of beginning work in Russia. When I came to think of it, I found I even begrudged the extra day; I was so keen to begin the work for which I had come so far. Marie took the news without excitement. She had met the Empress before as she was the niece of one of the ladies-in-waiting and had been to the Palace several times.

The next afternoon the General and the car arrived together and we drove to the Palace of Gatchina, a little way out of the city, between the White Lake and the Black Lake. We were escorted upstairs by footmen with plumed hats and red capes with little black eagles embroidered on them, to a cheerful English-looking drawing-room where the Empress was sitting writing.

I shall always be glad to have had that interview with one of the most delightful people I have ever met. Some royalties give the impression of hurry as if they, hard-pressed, were already half-way to their next engagement. Not so Marie Federovna. Royal to her fingertips, racy, forceful, amusing, she was something more. I think she had a maternal quality, and it left me with a sense of reassurance and comfort. She asked me a great many questions about Belgium, and I talked to her freely and told her how anxious I was to begin work.

"I am going to send you to some very old friends of mine," she said at the end of the interview. "Prince and Princess Volkonsky. They have a First Aid ambulance unit; they call it the 'Flying Ambulance', and they are doing the most splendid work at the front with Ivanov's army in Poland. I will speak to the Director of the Red Cross about it, and he will make all the arrangements."

I hugged myself with joy; I never imagined I should have been sent to anything so interesting.

"I should like that very much indeed, Ma'am. I hope it will be very soon."

She looked amused. "A very impatient person, I see. But first you must have a little training, and also learn some Russian. I shall arrange for you to go to the Smolny Institute where our Sisters of Mercy are prepared for the work at the front." She turned to Marie and smiled at her, "And as for you, my dear, I think it would be very helpful if you went to the Smolny too for a month or so. Your aunt told me it was some time since you had your classes, and the training at the Smolny is very practical."

I was delighted; I liked Marie very much, she was so pretty and sweet, and I should have felt very strange if I had had to go off to this training place alone.

The Empress talked to Marie for a few minutes in Russian and then called the General to her side and talked to him, and soon we were told to say goodbye.

"I shall look for news of you," the Empress said as we were making our deep courtesies, "God bless you and thank you for coming to Russia." She laid her hand on my shoulder, and with my whole heart I vowed to serve Russia if I could.

We were not due at the Smolny Convent until the next afternoon and there were two things I wanted to do. The letter from the Belgian woman to her husband was the most important. The address was on the envelope, but I must find out how far it was and ask Marie if she would come with me.

One of the clerks at the reception desk could speak English so I ran down to the hall and showed him the envelope, and asked him if he knew the name.

"Oh yes, he has been here nearly a year. He is a teacher of English, and he and his wife live quite near us."

"But his wife is in Brussels!"

"No, I assure you Madam, they have a little flat just across the road from us."

I showed him the envelope, "His wife gave me this letter for him."

"Then I am afraid he has two wives, Madam," grinned the clerk.

I was so furious at having carried this letter through Europe at the risk of being arrested, that I threw the letter into the hotel post-box, not knowing or caring if he ever got it.

Marie was tickled at my rage. "Never carry letters, my dear," she said, hooting with laughter, "you are very lucky not to be in prison."

The other thing I had to do was to make myself known at the British Embassy. Sir George Buchanan was our Ambassador at the time, and both he and Lady Georgina were enormously kind to me. I was made free of the Embassy and invited to come whenever I could. They asked me to be sure and keep in touch with them and to let them know when I left Petrograd. They knew and liked the Volkonskys and were delighted to hear I was going to work in their unit.

The next day we went to the Smolny Convent. It was a beautiful building designed by Rastrelli in the time of Elizabeth, daughter of Peter the Great. It was a fashionable convent school for daughters of noblemen until the war, when it was converted into a military hospital. The ballroom, where the noble maidens used to dance with very carefully chosen partners, was now filled with wounded soldiers. This was also the training school for the Red Cross sisters, who are called Sisters of Mercy in Russia. At the time we arrived there was a special course of instruction going on for those sisters who were to work at the front, and we were very lucky in having missed only a few days of this.

This hospital was a cheery, happy place. I specially loved the evenings when, before supper, the convalescent patients would sit together and sing. Sometimes it was their marching songs which made one's feet dance, sometimes folk songs from their own province; most often Cossack love songs, which Colonel Federov – swinging round in his wheel chair – used to accompany on his balalaika.

The royal princesses Anastasia, Maria, and the pretty gay Tatiana used to come in sometimes to chat with the patients or help with the bandaging. The Empress came once, and I was presented to her by the Directrice. She had the most tragic face I have ever seen, moving like the heroine of a Greek tragedy towards her inevitable fate. Later on, when I heard the horrifying news of the murder of the entire royal party in the cellars of Yekaterinburg, I could not help being glad that she had finished with the sorrows of her life and was at rest at last.

The practical work of the hospital was not difficult. Mostly dressings and bandaging and sterilising instruments, but it was bewildering to hear the rattle of Russian going on all round, and terribly worrying not to understand what the soldiers were asking for. Most of the sisters spoke French and a few who had had an English nanny or governess, spoke English. Marie, having been at school in England, was still thrilled to be talking to an English girl. She was very happy to be at the Smolny as she had a boyfriend who was a cadet taking his officer's course in Petrograd. Vladimir was working very hard and was only free in the evening so they had little time together. But Marie was wonderfully patient with my ignorance, giving up much of her spare time in translating the Russian lectures for me. She was a sensitive creature, easily hurt, not nearly as tough as my other Mary. I never meant to criticise, but at home I was accustomed to being very outspoken. I was intensely interested in the new life, and I dare say I asked indiscreet questions. But these were the tiniest ripples on what later became a great friendship.

There were not many spare moments at the Smolny, but I loved the rare autumn afternoons when Marie and I were free and could go for long walks together exploring the city. Petrograd is not one of the cities whose charms steal on one unawares. It is immense, arresting, insistently thrusting itself on one's imagination; a colossal city built for giants. It reminded me a little of Italy. The palaces, built of huge, giant blocks like the Strozzi palace in Florence, dominate the city. Splendid churches with cupolas of viridian green copper, or domes of azure-blue almost dwarfing St.Peters. We visited St.Isaac's Church one afternoon. It was full of people kneeling behind the golden screen, whispering prayers, imploring, weeping, pleading for the safety of their husbands and sons. Some convalescent soldiers were standing by a pillar praying too; the church was full of an insistent atmosphere of prayer. Now it is a museum, but I should not think all the antigod museums in the world could wholly destroy that atmosphere.

Another impression was the fantastic colouring of the buildings, gay mediterranean colours to warm this icy month. I especially loved the Admiralty, painted a spring daffodil yellow, sharp and discordant against the ash grey sky and ice blue snow. The Nevsky Prospekt is the main street and here are the most elegant shops. At this early period of the war they were still gay with fruit and flowers (mostly artificial, I admit) and hand-painted furnishings left over from happier times. Even embroidered peasant costumes were still seen in the windows, but there were no buyers; the shops were nearly empty.

I liked watching the passing crowd as much as anything else. Orthodox priests in black robes with their hair pinned up in a bun under a black head-dress, the sleigh drivers called istvoschiks, nearly all immensely fat, and looking even fatter than they really were, wrapped up to the chin in thick blue wadded coats and fur capes. Nannies with long brilliant ribbons fluttering from their caps, seeking the winter sunshine for their charges, a stream of humanity passing along, they all held a never ending interest for me.

It was not as cold here as in Finland, but great clumps of ice were swirling down the river Neva. Soon it would be frozen and quite immobile, but now, pale in the autumn mist, it stretched away into infinity.

We were walking there one afternoon, Marie pointing out the slender spires of the fortress of St.Peter and St.Paul on the opposite bank. I remembered a black and red book at home with stories of innocent prisoners dragging their chains over the snow, or measuring out their life in fetid dungeons in the same fortress that faced us now, standing out black against the saffron yellow of the sunset. Boats were moored at the steps of the Watergate, the entrance to the underground cells where the prisoners must have entered.

I shivered, "Are there any prisoners there now?" I asked Marie.

"I shouldn't think so. Unless perhaps some political ones; the others would be fighting."

I suppose I looked incredulous, for Marie very unexpectedly lost her temper. "Foreigners never understand us," the little patriot said furiously. "Just as long as war is on Russian soil, we would fight to the last inhabitant. We should never permit those German devils to win; we shall go on until they are down on their knees begging for mercy."

"Yes, but Marie, everyone says that thousands of soldiers or millions if you like, aren't much use without millions of guns too, and you are terribly short of them."

"That is not true at all. Already we are beginning to win. They nearly reached Warsaw you know in the first days, and now we have pushed them back into Germany. I know the foreign press accuses us of all sorts of corruption, but as my father said the other day, you have only to go to the station here and see all the trucks and supplies for the front." This sounded marvellous; I pictured myself hastening to Germany with the victorious troops.

I said something to Marie about going to Poland soon, but she shook her head.

"You will never be allowed to go to the front, my dear. No foreigners are allowed anywhere near the front. I expect they will put you in one of the military hospitals here or in Moscow. It would have been nice if we could have gone together. I have enjoyed our little excursions. It has been so good to speak English again; I shall miss you.

I did not like to remind her of what the Empress had said, especially as there had been no word from Prince Volkonsky. Perhaps they, too, did not like to have 'foreigners' in their unit. I did not mind very much; I was ready to help at the front or at the back.

We went back to the Smolny, and Marie was very much surprised when the dvornik rushed at us and said we were to go to the Directrice's office at once. I had only seen her twice before – the night of our arrival, and when she presented me to the Empress. We hurried upstairs and found her sitting at her table with the Director of the Red Cross beside her. She motioned us to sit. She told us that a raging battle had been going on in Poland for some days, and there were a great number of wounded. The twelve of us who had been taking the course at Smolny were to go off to the front at once, ten to the Grand Duchess Anastasia's Hospital, and two of us – Marie and myself – were to go to Prince Volkonsky's mobile unit.

I was bubbling over with joy because Marie and I were going together, but she gave me a friendly kick on the ankle, and I realised in time that this was a solemn and ceremonious occasion. Every time a group of Sisters of Mercy were sent off to the front, there was a special service for them in the chapel, and the farewell service would take place in half-an-

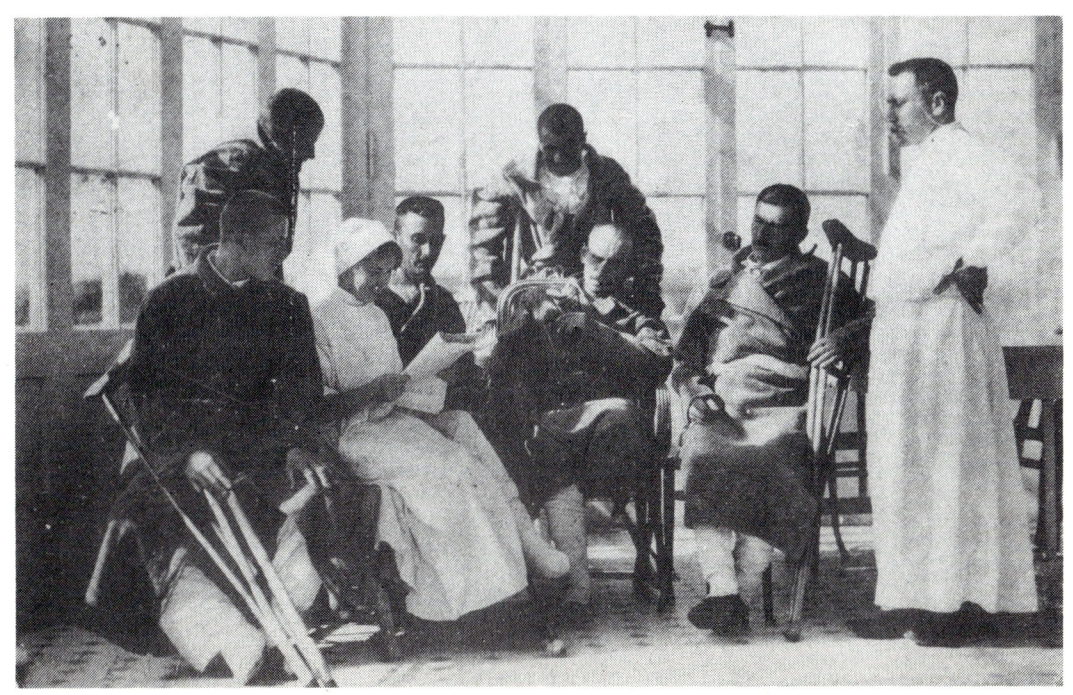

A Russian Hospital

A Refugee

hour, so we had to hurry and get ready.

When I arrived in the chapel, the Directrice was in her stall, and the church was filled with white-clad sisters. The priest came out of the golden door that separated the congregation from the inner sanctuary, raised his arms, and made a great sweeping sign of the Cross, and the service began.

It was very moving. There were no lights except from the silver candelabra on the altar, and the candles burning in front of the ikons, but there were a great many of these. The walls were glowing like old tapestries, faded crimson, blue and gold. The red vestments of the priest caught the light of the altar candles and looked like a stained glass window. I could not understand the words, but I felt the solemnity of the occasion. We were going into danger, some of us might perhaps not return, but it was wonderful to feel one had been chosen – and I prayed that my help would be accepted. We were dismissed with a blessing for ourselves and for our future work.

The journey to Petrograd may have been a bit grim, but the one to Warsaw was a nightmare. I never thought that any train could be so burstingly full. When we left the station, there were even a few men standing on the step outside. As the train gained momentum, their agonised faces signalled to us for help. It was difficult to open the door, but they managed somehow, and all were pulled in, except one oldish man who fell back heavily on the line.

There were soldiers everywhere. It was impossible to push one's way down the corridor at all; some even slept on the floor in the lavatory. Those standing outside the carriage blocked all the light from the window, and the fug hung about like a miasma. When the train stopped at the stations and the door opened, people fell out on to the platform, compact as a swarm of bees, and gasped like fishes in the pure fresh air.

We took nearly four days to get to Warsaw, and the nearer we got, the worse the crowding, as masses more soldiers pushed their way in. The officers who accompanied them looked grave and preoccupied. They would not tell us much, but it seemed that a big battle was in progress in front of Lodz, and that the Russians were falling slowly back towards Warsaw. The losses must have been very heavy; we saw line upon line of ambulance trains going in the opposite direction.

Marie looked dispirited and tired. Her easy optimism had disappeared.

We were met at the Warsaw station by a man in Red Cross uniform. No one knew at the moment where Prince Volkonsky's unit was, so I was sent with Marie to a big military hospital near the station.

The staff of the hospital met us with open arms. They were nearly distracted with the numbers of wounded being brought in. The improvised wards were quite full and they had begun to put two wounded into one bed, head to tail. The Directrice was worried; she did not know where to put us to sleep. We, too, were nearly dead on our feet and had been thinking of a warm wash and clean clothes, but evidently neither of these luxuries would be forthcoming in this crisis.

The building had been a large day college, and there were only a few basins in the adjoining annexe. The Directrice reflected for a moment and then took us to a small room where several of the sisters were sleeping on the floor on straw palliasses. With angelic patience they moved up closer together to make room for us, and we lay down between them just as we were. They must have been wildly uncomfortable, but never by word or deed did they let us see it.

We did not rest for very long. The wounded were still being carried in from the station, so we were roused and set to work to fill some more palliasse covers with straw and lay them along the corridor. As fast as possible the wounded were carried to the operating room on stretchers, and then back to us in the corridor to be looked after.

The next day, Marie and I were sent to work in the bandaging room. All day long the broken men were being brought in to have their wounds dressed. Smashed heads, bodies, faces and limbs. There was no limit to the human misery, no limit either to the fortitude with which they bore their pain.

I might have expected to be frightened, but there was no time for that. This was a very different affair from Petrograd. At the Smolny hospital there were cheery patients, plenty of nurses to look after them, and comforts - even little luxuries for those who needed them. Here there was nothing. Imagine being restless and in pain, perhaps sick after an operation, and not even having a bed to oneself!

Unfortunately, the first effect of this on me was to forget entirely the Russian I had learned so laboriously at Smolny. I could not remember the simplest word, and the first week was a nightmare because I did not understand quickly what I was supposed to do. It was not until after about ten days that suddenly I began to see daylight and could at least understand quickly the gist of a muttered request from a patient.

We worked all day and we worked all night, more or less, bandaging and changing dressings. And when the exhausted porters had trundled out the last stretcher, we had to cut and prepare the dressings for the next day.

The wards were untidy and dirty, the patients overcrowded, the food was poor and the staff cruelly overworked, but for sheer devotion there was never a hospital like it. We were too few in numbers to have a permanent night sister. We all used to take it in turns, three by three each night. That worked out about once a week in theory but not in practice. Night after night, when we heard a new convoy of wounded being brought in, I woke to see sister after sister rise and, dressing silently, slip off for a few hours to help. For very shame I could do no less. Personally, I found the night on duty hell, sandwiched as it was between two hard days, but the Russian sisters never faltered.

The Directrice, or Sister Superior, as she was called here, was the heart of the hospital. She was small and would have been rather plain except for her large humorous mouth and wide-set dark blue eyes, which could sum one up at times in a most disconcerting fashion. She knew the world and mankind very well. She had been a spoilt debutante at the court in her youthful days, a Sister of Mercy in the Russo-Japanese war, head of a convent in Moscow, and now Directrice here with a great hospital to control. She could not be taken in, either by fool or knave, and she always had comfort to give the sinful and suffering, and an inward fount of calm which nothing could disturb. There was one night when a message came to say that four hundred wounded were on their way and would arrive immediately. The sisters were flapping about like hens wondering where on earth we could put them all, until Sister Superior came along and, in two minutes, there was perfect calm. Under her direction we collected all the stretchers and filled palliasses, boiled instruments, and prepared dressings. The four hundred arrived about midnight, were examined and made comfortable without any fuss. Each man was undressed on the stretcher, examined by the surgeon, (we had borrowed two from another hospital), and the head sister dressed his wounds. We put on a clean shirt and pants, a blanket over him, and left him to rest. The sister in charge of the kitchen and her assistants stayed up all night in order to give each man who could take it a bowl of soup. Dear Sister Superior stayed all night with the dying, writing letters home for them, and comforting them as only she could do.

When a great crisis in my own life happened later on, I longed to be able to go to her and get comfort, but she had left us then. She died a few weeks after we left Warsaw, of sheer overwork.

We only heard scraps of news from the doctors, and even the patients who came straight from the front did not know much. But it could not be concealed that the situation was very grave, and they spoke of frightful fighting near a town called Lodz, so that the troops must have retreated already a very long way from the frontier.

50

Warsaw was full of reinforcements. We sometimes saw them marching in, fine big men who looked as though they could give a good account of themselves. The Russian soldier is not very self-conscious. He generally jingles with pots and pans hung round his person like an animated Christmas tree, and will wrap a shawl round his head if he is cold, whether he is in the most elegant street in Warsaw, or in a frozen trench.

There was at that time a great devotion between the officers and men. One day an orderly brought his wounded officer to the hospital. He was a delicate looking boy with a bullet through his lung. The orderly would not leave him and would hardly let us touch him, not that there was much to be done. The boy was obviously dying when he was brought to us. The orderly stayed by his side until he died and then burst into tears he had restrained for so long. Flinging himself over his officer's body, he implored God to let him die too.

The news remained bad. Lodz was just holding out, but it was entirely surrounded by the enemy and they were not able to evacuate any of the wounded. We had orders to clear the hospital as far as we could to receive them when they came, but the beds remained empty and we got a little rest, thank goodness!

One Sunday afternoon, Marie and I went round to the Bristol hotel to see if there were any English papers to be had. There were none, and I felt very, very far away from home; it seemed an eternity since I had had news of my family. Nothing had come through since I had left Copenhagen.

We returned to the hospital, and were told to go straight back to the Hotel Bristol. Prince Peter Volkonsky had arrived in Warsaw and wanted to see us.

He was sitting writing at a table in the hall, and I took a good look at him before he saw us. He looked like a prince out of a fairy tale. An immensely tall man, emaciated but very handsome, with a beaked nose like an eagle, fiercely arching eyebrows, very alarming indeed until one knew him. This was the man I was going to work under for the rest of the time I was in Russia.

It was never his way to impart information, but he did say a few words about the unit. It belonged to the Second Army under General Ivanov, who had several mobile ambulance units under his command. Ours was the smallest and was very mobile; it was called a Flying Field Ambulance, with five ambulances and twenty sanitars (medical orderlies) and drivers to pick up the wounded and transport them to the nearest field hospital, and another ambulance with surgical supplies in which we travelled ourselves. There was also a surgeon for each ambulance, except ours. And, lastly, Prince Peter's own body servant, Julian, our rock and stay in every emergency.

Lodz, the large town where the army was covering the Warsaw defences, was in great danger, but still held. We were going there the next day, Prince Peter said, so would we be ready to start very early in the morning. He indicated that the interview was over, smiled and put out his hand, and that was that.

The night was peaceful for once, but I was too excited to sleep. I was thrilled to become a member of the Volkonsky Flying Field Ambulance.

It was still pitch dark when Nicholas called us to begin loading the ambulance with the blankets and medical supplies that Prince Peter had been collecting in Warsaw. It was freezing hard and our hands were so numb that we finished loading later than we expected. We had brought very little of our personal stuff, Nicholas had told us the evening before that Prince Peter had a kink about luggage; he could not bear us to have more than the smallest case of our own. Wishing to be helpful, I had left most of my possessions at the Hotel Bristol hoping to pick them up next time the ambulance came into Warsaw to get supplies. This was an act I soon bitterly regretted as the Arctic wind blew through my thin coat. Even so, we were terribly overcrowded at the back where the knobs of the big steriliser stuck into my spine whenever I leaned back. But we finished at last, and with no time for breakfast, we set out for Lodz.

Nicholas was driving; Prince Peter, stern and unapproachable, sat beside him; Marie and I in the cramped space at the back. It was about 200 kilometres to Lodz, they said, but it took nearly all day to get there.

When the war first began, the Germans advanced almost to Warsaw and then had to retreat again to beyond the Prussian frontier. As they fell back, they destroyed nearly all the bridges and most of the roads, so we had to make constant detours. In England we should have called the roads that remained impassable, but troops were marching up them all the time. This considerably impeded our progress, but I found it very interesting to watch them. There was a regiment of Cossacks in front of us for a long time and, when at last we got by, we were tangled up with a Remount Detachment with hundreds of Siberian ponies with thick yellow coats and long dark manes. We met them later on; they were darlings, perfectly tame and as obedient as dogs. But on this occasion, never having encountered an automobile before, the entrancing creatures were curvetting and dancing all over the road.

Lunch time came and went, but Prince Peter gave no sign to stop. Nicholas grinned at Marie once or twice when we were halted for a moment, pointed to his stomach and shook his head. The second time, he threw us over a packet of cigarettes. One of these helped, but by no means alleviated the gaping void in my inside — Russian cigarettes are three quarters cardboard!

Presently, we heard the dull rumble of guns, rather like a far off thunderstorm. I knew we must be getting near. The going began to be very difficult and there was great confusion on the road, civilians trying to get out, and troops trying to force their way in. There were shell craters everywhere, very difficult in the half light for the ambulance to avoid, over-turned wagons — their contents spilling into the awful slimy mud — and dead horses lay about with their legs sticking starkly towards the sky.

As the dusk was greying into night, we struggled into the city of Lodz, a large manufacturing town, the Manchester of Poland, they called it. It would be an unlovely town even in peacetime. It looked unspeakably miserable now with window-less facades and crumbling ruins.

Lodz had a very large Jewish population, and the streets were crowded. The shops were open but there was nothing in them — a few dummy tins on a shelf, and a few frozen vegetables. Forlorn women with children hanging on to their skirts were coming out of them with empty baskets; men, pale as mushrooms, with old-fashioned side curls framing their faces, dressed in shabby black kaftans, were slinking along the street. The ambulance edged its way through the crowd until it reached the big day school which our unit had taken over as a dressing station.

We were taken to a small office and introduced to Princess Volkonsky. She knew Marie Ivanova's aunt at the Court and kissed her warmly, greeted me charmingly and said how glad she was that I had come. I felt at home with her at once; she was very easy to get on with. She was the greatest contrast to her alarming husband that could be imagined, small, fair, vivacious, and full of fun. She had had English nurses and governesses in her childhood, and spoke English as well as I, which was a great comfort. I think she was glad to relax for a few minutes and called Julian to bring tea. He immediately brought glasses of pale sugarless tea, but nothing to eat. Princess asked him if they had not brought any bread from Warsaw. He shook his head. She seemed very disappointed and called out, "Peter, it can't be you have forgotten the bread!"

"Very sorry, darling, but there was so much to do in Warsaw that I forgot all about it. But there are plenty of biscuits," he added consolingly, and told Julian to bring some.

Marie made a face when they came. I had never eaten dog biscuits, but that is what they looked like. Nevertheless, we were so hungry that we managed to eat some while Princess began to tell us something about the unit.

"We only arrived here ourselves the day before yesterday, to relieve the Novgorodski Unit," she explained. "They had been here only a few days getting the place ready, but they had sudden orders to move and we were sent to take over at a moment's notice. They took their ambulances and all their supplies with them. The wounded have been coming in ever since. The Prince says there are about twelve thousand wounded in the town. Lodz is nothing but a big hospital. The walking have to be taken to civilians' homes; there isn't room for them in the hospitals. They can't evacuate them by train because the Germans have got the railway. There is only one road open, the one you have just come by, and that is wanted for troops."

"I suppose that's why we had so few patients in Warsaw," Marie said. "We kept on hearing about the dreadful battles round Lodz, and we cleared out our big hospital for them, but they never came."

"Oh, you have been in Warsaw," Princess replied, "that is very interesting. You will be able to tell me something I have been wanting to know for some time. Is Grand Duchess Anastasia's Hospital there yet?"

Marie opened her mouth to say she had not heard, when a noise like an express train reverberated just over our heads and made us jump. It burst somewhere near, and the whole house shook, but Princess did not seem very worried.

"Oh, they have begun again," was all she said. "They started at this time last night; I am afraid we are going to be very busy again."

A second explosion followed and this time Princess got up. "I must go, but you can both come with me and see the hospital if you like, while there is still daylight."

Our unit had taken over what had been the high school. Upstairs there were large light class rooms, and these had been prepared as wards, but when the bombardment began, they dared not put the patients there, and carried them all down to the ground floor and the basement. This school basement had evidently been used as a gymnasium. Ladders and

55

trapezes and vaulting horses were still in place. The ground floor was composed of little wooden cubicles, each containing a piano and a chair.

"How cold!" Marie exclaimed involuntarily.

It was frightfully cold. The gas was half frozen and gave only a feeble flicker. There was no heating, no wood, and no coal in Lodz. There was indeed nothing at all in Lodz.

"My husband went to Warsaw to get some blankets," Princess remarked, "and brought you both back as well as the blankets. We are so glad to see them; we shall distribute them directly."

The stretcher-bearers were carrying their burdens very carefully down the narrow stairs and in the bare, dingy surroundings the medical orderlies were laying down straw.

"We are going to open this as another ward," Princess explained. "Perhaps you and your little English friend would like to take it over between you."

Even as she spoke, familiar looking stretchers and groaning men were being edged through the narrow door, so we went no further, but threw off our coats, collected some overalls from a pile and set to work.

The night was pure hell!

They were bringing in the wounded the whole time. Most of them were very bad cases and had not had their wounds attended to since they, or one of their comrades, had put on the first-aid dressing, and their wounds stank when we pulled off filthy bits of lint.

The men came in soaked with blood and covered with vermin, but as they came in, so they had to lie, we had no shirts or pants for them. They lay on the straw, trembling with cold until Julian came round with the army blankets we had brought from Warsaw. There was only one for each man, but at least they were clean and warm and dry.

The unit surgeon, Basil Petrov, looked in and said he would come and operate in a few minutes and left a case of instruments to be boiled, so Julian and Nicholas brought down the big sterilizer we had brought with us. This was to be my special job, both here and at all the other places we worked in. I tried to start it, but it was difficult to find enough water to keep it going. There was only a cold tap down here, and that was broken and the connecting pipe burst, but a tiny drip from that made a streamlet that trickled into the ward all night. There was a row of lavatories, but they had all frozen too. The broken chains dangled loose, and when the lavatory bowl was full, there was nothing to do but empty the enamel slop pail, which was the only utensil we had, out of the window. This brought howls of dismay from everyone as the icy draughts blew in from the courtyard.

At midnight, we stopped for a few minutes when Princess called us for a meal. Another ambulance had just come in from Warsaw, and among the supplies was a packet of bread and a bottle of wine for Princess. I thought I was too tired to eat, but the wine gave us all new energy. We needed that wine; all night long the procession of broken bodies came in and were laid gently on the straw. All night, the surgeon worked at the improvised operating table, amputating legs and arms, stitching up wounds, probing for bullets. All night we carried on where the surgeon left off, bandaging wounds, sterilising instruments, cutting off filthy uniforms, until I felt if one more stretcher came in, I could not go on. But they came in all the same, and somehow or other we managed to carry on.

Early in the morning there was a blessed lull, and Marie and I lay down on a stretcher and were dead to the world before our heads touched the pillow.

We did not sleep very long, another convoy of wounded arrived. Even as we got up, a few of the men were being carried in. At five in the morning there was another pause, and Marie and I relaxed again on our stretchers, our ears deaf to the sound of guns, our eyes closed as we lay down. The orderlies called us again in an hour's time; another batch of very badly wounded men was being brought in – some of them were dead already; many died in an hour or two.

If...if...if we had had hot water bottles, hot blankets, hot drinks, we could have saved some of them perhaps.

The bombardments began again, the hospital clock tower was hit, but we were too busy and too tired to heed it.

At daylight came breakfast. The orderlies came in with white enamel slop pails filled with hot weak tea, and biscuits sopped with tea for those who could take it. We had a pause ourselves – we stopped and sat down for a few minutes on the packing cases. Afterwards we wanted to make the men more comfortable but there was very little we could do. We had seventy men by now in our ward, lying on the straw. There was only one basin and one towel so we could not wash them, and anyway we felt it was too cold to expose them. Some of the new army blankets were already spoilt with blood, the nice new army blankets were crawling with lice and other horrors. There were plenty of cigarettes, thank God: the Russian variety may be mostly cardboard, but a lot of comfort was got out of them.

57

Doctor Petrov came along to dress some of the worst cases; he had been working all night and was nearly at the end of his tether. He sat down with his head in his hands and had two minutes' sleep between each case, while we took off the dirty bandages.

Princess looked in to tell us the news. The Germans were closing in on the town and the road we had come up was now under fire. Nobody could go in and nobody could get out. But still, ceaselessly, the stretcher-bearers entered, bringing in more wounded, many German now, as well as Russian. They were furious to find themselves prisoners, and were sulky and discontented whatever one did for them. We realised acutely that it looked very much as if we were going to be prisoners ourselves too, before very long.

We were getting very short of chloroform; the men to be operated on could only have a few whiffs to take the edge off their pain. Still worse, we were nearly out of anti-tetanus serum and that meant that a lot of our wounded would have to die a very painful death. Dressings and bandages were very short too, and the wounds got more and more foul, and the ward smelled worse as time went on. The guns never seemed to stop. A great part of the town was destroyed; the hospital roof was hit, but there were no casualties.

They started bringing in wounded civilians, but after the first batch Prince Peter had to give orders to refuse them, there simply was not any more room. That evening, when we went to supper, even the hall was full of all lying on the floor. An old Jewish woman lay on a stretcher, both her legs blown off. She had no pain, only lamented that she had lost her wig. She died a few minutes later, clasping her bald head.

I cannot remember how long the siege of Lodz lasted. It seemed to be years and years – an eternity. Time did not count any more. We were all so tired that nothing seemed to matter. If anyone spoke to us, it took a long time for the words to penetrate. We were as dirty, as lice-ridden and as thin as the patients.

Princess began taking us to the hotel for our midday meal. Though I always felt guilty at having better food than the patients, at least we got some fresh air and food of a kind, though there was no bread and no sugar, but anyway the tea was not served from an enamel pail.

The outings were spoilt by the famished children in the street who tugged at our clothes and whined for food. I always saved some of my supper biscuits for them, but it didn't go far.

58

So time went on and on – the eternal procession of wounded the dirt and the vermin, and by far the worst – the terrible smell of death and rot.

I was not homesick. I could not remember any other life. I was always hungry, and would have given all I had possessed for something sweet.

The drivers now helped in the wards as all the ambulances were immobile. Nicky got himself attached to our ward; I cannot imagine what we should have done without him. He never seemed to be tired or to want any sleep, always scrounging round to find things for us, teasing us until we could have beaten him, howling with laughter every time he heard me speaking Russian, and betting everything he possessed that the war would be over before Christmas. He once came prancing in with a present for me. It was a pink soap doll he had found in an empty shop. He had thought it was sugar, bless his heart.

One afternoon, while we were waiting for another convoy, he showed me a photograph of his home in the Ukraine. It was a delightful old manor house, rather like an English country house. His father had married the daughter of a neighbouring Polish nobleman, and it was from his mother that Nicholas had inherited his gaiety and good looks, also his religion as he had been brought up as a Uniate, or Catholic Orthodox.

A few days after a very severe night attack, things began to happen. Some Russian soldiers arrived out of nowhere and announced that they had come to relieve us for a few hours. I can never explain to anyone what it meant to be able to sleep and sleep and sleep. But before we had really had enough, we were awakened by ear-splitting crashes and bangs very close. We were used to the ordinary sounds of the guns, but this was something special. We got up at once just as Prince Peter came in. He brought news. The Russian army had succeeded in taking the railway station. He didn't think they would be able to hold it for many hours, but in the meantime the road to Warsaw was open. The army was getting up railway trucks as fast as possible, and all the wounded were to be evacuated immediately in charge of the sisters who had been relieving us. Carts were being commandeered and would come up and down between the hospital and the station all night.

We worked very hard. At first we tried to give each man a clean dressing, but we soon ran out of them, and all we could do was to wrap them in their army blankets and hope that it would not be too long before they got back to base. There were a few wounded who were dying and could not be moved. Early next morning, everybody, except these pitiful few, had been taken down to the station. We knew now that the Russians would have to give up Lodz very soon, and I could not bear the thought that we should have to hand over our precious wounded to the victorious German army. I saw Nicky passing under the window, whistling as usual.

"Nicky!" I called.

"What can I do for our Violetta?" He stepped over the window-sill into the ward.

"Nicky, what about the men who can't go? Surely they won't be left here all alone?"

"No," he answered gruffly, "Vladimir is going to stay."

I found out afterwards that they had all offered to stay and had drawn lots.

"I am terribly unhappy about them. And if the wretched Vladimir stays, surely he will be a prisoner."

"I expect he will manage to get out; Vladimir is a pretty cunning character," he said comfortingly. "Look, Violetta, I have an idea. You know German. Can't you write a ticket with each man's name on it, and a note asking the Germans to be kind to them?"

"Oh yes, I will. Where can we find some paper?"

"Masses of school reports in the drawer in the office, I'll get some."

He wrote the names of the soldiers and pinned them on to their shirts.

Nicky didn't know any German and I had half forgotten mine. We composed a little note. I still have the copy on a dirty old report sheet.

'Deutschen soldaten. Bitte seien sie barmhertzig für diesen armen Menschen. Sie sind soldaten wie euch, sie sind stark verwündert und können nicht lang leben.'

I hoped the Germans would understand my rather peculiar grammar. This done, Nicky turned to go.

"Wait a second, Nick. Do you think you could help me get this loathsome straw into the yard and burn it?"

"Don't you touch it. I'll get some of the sanitars, and we'll cart the beastly stuff out and make a bonfire."

Princess, seeing a thick pall of black smoke coming from below, was rather alarmed and came to see what was happening. We were as black as tinners, and when the very charming Polish lady, who was with Princess, saw us, amusement struggled with politeness and they both convulsed with laughter. Princess introduced her as Panna Wanda Filipski. She had a country house just outside Lodz, and had come to invite us to a bath, a meal and a bed in her house. What a heavenly invitation!

So, in the afternoon, Princess, Marie and I, with Basil Petrov and one of the drivers, started off for Panna Wanda's house. It was horrible, leaving poor Vladimir and the dying patients who were Russian, but we were ordered to leave, so it had to be done. The few Germans who were wounded and could not be moved, were overjoyed to think their compatriots would soon release them.

The house was about half a mile away. The 'ambus' (as we called them) were all out, so we had to walk, and we were in such a state of fatigue that it took all our courage to do it. We had not had a bath, or taken off our clothes, since we had come to Lodz, and were nearly as verminous as our patients. We had not had more than two hours' consecutive sleep at a time; our food was of the scantiest, so we were all feeling like death now that we had stopped at last.

We had a marvellous welcome when we arrived. After Panna Wanda had greeted us, her old nanny caught me by the arm and took me off to a bathroom. There was a sponge and soap, and I lay blissfully soaking in the hot water while she tut-tutted over my horrible clothes, and finally took them away and sponged them and pressed them. When she brought them back, she had added a chemise, fine and soft and smelling of verbena, which must have belonged to her mistress. It was voluminous and fell in folds around me, but it was heaven to be clean again. I dressed and went along to the dining-room where the others were waiting for me, complaining bitterly that I had been so slow. There was a white table cloth on that table, there were candles in shining silver holders burning on it, there was a fragrant smell of coffee, and a maid was just bringing in an enormous omelette. We sat down, looked wolfishly at our plates, and picked up our knives and forks.

Prince Peter strode in, grey-faced. He gave a brief greeting to our hostess, then turned to us and said we must go. "No, Peter," Princess said, "we must eat first. Do come and sit down."

He stood there, tall as a pine tree, with a great cape, glistening with snow, over his shoulders.

"You must come immediately. Are all you people deaf? Don't you hear the rifle fire? The Germans are already all over the north part of the town. We have orders to leave at once."

"But, Peter!"

61

"At once!" he repeated, and meekly we put down our knives and forks, gave a last look at that beautiful meal, and with mournful thanks to our hostess, followed him out into the night, she protesting vigorously.

"Hurry!" Prince Peter ordered us. "The ambulance is waiting for us at the hotel."

But when we got to the hotel, our 'ambu' was not there.

"It has just gone away, Excellency," the hotel manager said; "it was filled with wounded officers."

Prince Peter seemed very pleased about that, much more pleased than we were, and ordered us to come in to the hotel and announced that we should have some supper. He unbent for once that night and teased me unmercifully, threatening to report me to General Ivanov for looking insubordinate when I was told to leave my supper and return to duty.

We went into the restaurant. At one end was the grand-stand where, in happier days, the orchestra had played gypsy music while the guests toyed with delicate food and wine from the buffet. Now, there was a great hole in it and the bandstand was overturned. The snow and wind beating through the room did not obscure the noise – the tack–tack–tack of machine-gun fire.

We sat down at a table with a list of noble vintages in front of us, lamenting the beautiful meal we had left, but the only fare the management could offer us was the eternal tea and some toasted crusts of bread.

We sat in the dining-room all night, too tired to care whether the Germans came or not. I found myself lying on Nick's shoulder when I awoke. He was very stiff and cross, and heaved me off, and then his sharp ears heard the note of our 'ambu' outside. We went to the door to look and there it was, with Pavel – one of our drivers – shouting that we had better hurry up unless we wanted to be prisoners. Prince Peter emerged from the hall and ordered us all to get in im-mediately, and we left Lodz by the back door, so to speak. A trail of bullets met us as we got to the edge of the town, and one of them embedded itself safely in the 'ambu' door. A golden dawn was just breaking with innocent little pink clouds proclaiming a lovely day, the bombing had stopped, and all looked calm and peaceful except for the main road crowded with fleeing refugees. Presently, we had to stop to change a wheel and we looked back. Lodz was burning! Great clouds of smoke were going up in columns. I thought of our poor wounded men that we had left behind, and of the plucky Vladimir with them. I prayed hard that he might escape and tried, but failed, to remember who was the patron saint of soldiers. I could not help being glad that it was Vladimir, and not Nicky, who had been left behind.

There were loud German aeroplanes waffling about over-head, so we did not dally once the wheel was changed. We left the crowded main road and turned into a very narrow side road; if anyone met us we could not have passed, but every-one was going the other way, as far as possible from the Germans, who were now in occupation of Lodz.

We bumped along until, at mid-day, we came to an inn. Prince Peter ordered Pavel to stop for a meal and we all trouped into the primitive dining place. Madam had only some rye bread and soup to give us, but it was a treat, not having had bread for so long.

The host told Prince Peter that he had some rare old Tokay wine down in his cellar, and he was told to bring it up at once. It tasted very good, light and mellow, but it must have been stronger than it appeared. We got into the 'ambu' again, I dissolved into space and knew nothing more until we got to Warsaw late that night.

Marie was shaking me. "Do wake up, Violetta. This is Warsaw."

"I feel awful, Marie. I wish I hadn't drunk that wine."

"Never mind. Here's the hotel, and we can go to bed and sleep for ever. Come on."

Stiff and sick, I stumbled over the step of the ambulance, and followed up the steps of the hotel. As we got inside the swing door, a tall woman, dressed as a sister of mercy darted forward and kissed the Princess on both cheeks.

"That is the Grand Duchess Anastasia." Marie whispered.

They embraced affectionately and stood talking and talking. Marie and I stood first on one foot and then on the other. The others crept away to bed, and I would have followed them if I had known where to go.

Presently Princess came towards us. She looked apologetic. "I want to present you both to the Grand Duchess. We were just not too far gone to drop a curtsey.

"The Grand Duchess is asking you to give a little help in her hospital tonight," Princess said. "I know you are both very tired, but there are so many wounded being brought in that the sisters are nearly distracted. Grand Duchess heard that we were coming tonight and she thought we could help her for a day or so."

I did not say anything, but I thought...I can't! I can't! and Marie can't either.

"I thought we might do one short shift tonight."

We hesitated, and then answered rather sulkily, "Yes, Princess."

"They are from Lodz," Princess said softly.

That was different. If they were our own dear wounded from Lodz, then gladly would we sit up another night, even if it killed us. We could see that Princess was very pleased, and we were glad then not to have let her down. Oh, but how were we going to get through the night?

"Violetta, "I heard Princess say, "You have been asleep

all the afternoon; perhaps you could take the first shift. I will take over from you at midnight."

I followed Grand Duchess Anastasia across to her hospital. She gave me over to a rather sharp-faced Russian sister, her face dead white, and her eyes staring with fatigue. She could not speak English, but luckily understood French. My Russian was still shaky.

"What shall I do, Sister?" I heard myself saying in a dream.

"If you would go to the linen room, please, and undo the bale of blankets, and then go round the ground floor where the worst cases are and give them each a blanket."

She indicated the linen room and I stumbled in. There were bales of blankets. I unpacked one. How delicious they looked! How clean and warm. What they would have meant to us at Lodz. I thought I would just sit down for five minutes before distributing them.

When I awoke, it was morning. I was lying across the bale of blankets; the others had all gone. Princess had taken over from me as she promised, and had mercifully let me lie. I slunk back to the Bristol, bitterly ashamed of myself, but if the whole German army had been behind me, I could not have kept awake.

We refitted and rested for a few days, then came orders from General Ivanov. The unit was to go to Skierniewice.

We started off in great style from Warsaw. The Grand Duchess and her staff gave us a good send off. We had helped them a great deal, and had taken it in turns to do night duty. I had not disgraced myself again!

We got to Skierniewice late that night after the usual hold-ups in seas of mud and snow. It was a small town, important only because the railways to Germany and Austria diverge there.

The Czar had a hunting box nearby in the middle of a pine forest and we were taking this over as a dressing station. There were no wounded and there did not appear to be any battle. For two days there was nothing to do but sleep and walk through the pine forest into Skierniewice for our meals. After the smells of Lodz, the forest smelt like the gate of heaven. Twice a day, at eleven a.m. and five p.m., we walked a couple of kilometres to the railway station. Believe it or not, a Central European restaurant was standing on the rails; this was our dining-room! The officers from a Defence Point nearby dined here too, so there were thirty or forty of us for meals, and it was enormous fun.

There was always something going on at the station. One day a line of trucks went through, filled to the top with trophies from the battlefield: swords, helmets, water bottles - everything. A soldier gave me a German helmet, but Prince Peter would not let me keep it. Another time a train brought up part of a regiment from Warsaw. Just as half of them had detrained four German aeroplanes spied it, came down as low as they dared, and began to machine-gun the troops. At once every soldier began firing off his rifle, and the officer roared orders not to waste ammunition.

We were having lunch when this infernal row began and we all threw down our knives and forks and rushed out to see what was happening. The aeroplane flew away as if the devil was after it. Fortunately, there was not much damage done.

Another time I saw a horrible sight. An old Jew had been caught in the act of spying; four soldiers were marching him to the station to be tried before the Tribunal in Warsaw. The old man still had the coloured paper in his hand with which he had been signalling. The crowd at the station were furious and set on him. They snatched him from the soldiers, and began to beat and kick him. The blood was pouring down his agonised face and he was shaking so badly that he could hardly stand, but there was no prayer for mercy. He probably knew that it was no use. The Tribunal was saved the trouble of condemning him! I suppose the old man's family was hungry and probably the Germans paid well, but the crowd was in no mind to make excuses for a spy caught red-handed.

Sometimes a train of prisoners passed. They were mostly Austrians and looked hopeless and starved. The sight of prisoners and the absence of gunfire made us hope that the tide of battle had begun to flow in the opposite direction for once.

One Sunday morning, Marie and I were walking along to the little Catholic church at the edge of the forest - Marie belonged to the Russian Orthodox Church, but as there were very few of these in Poland, she generally came with me. It was plain to see that another battle was pending. Numerous batteries went through the forest, each drawn by eight stalwart horses. It was hard work for them and for us too, for we were over the ankles in the mixture of mud and snow. The guns were followed by a company of Siberian Cossacks, wild-looking creatures with great goatskin capes, black fur caps and long lances. One of them had his little son with him. The boy could not have been more than ten or eleven, but he was riding his pony so proudly, valiantly trying to keep up with his father. We often had quite young boys brought in wounded, especially

Cossacks. They were regimental pets, being used for runners or messengers.

Other troops were coming up behind the Siberians - Tartars, Caucasians, Little Russians and Russians from Turkestan.

"Do you remember what we were talking about in Petrograd, Marie? Here are the men, but where are the supplies? They will all be killed presently."

"Stop! Stop!" burst out Marie, the tears running down her cheeks. "I can't imagine what has happened. Something must have gone terribly wrong. I don't know why they can't get the things up to the front. Russia is so large, so rich, and everybody is giving thousands of roubles for the war. All the supplies must be somewhere. It is frightful for General Ivanov not to have enough guns. We never hear much firing from our side, and half the regulars have no guns; they are told to pick up the dead men's rifles."

I did not go on with the discussion because I could see how distressed Marie was, but even I, who knew nothing of war, could see how badly everything was going for us. I wished passionately that I knew how it was going with our own troops. While in Petrograd, I had seen the English papers at the Embassy, but that was some time ago: I had had no news since.

When we got to church, it was crammed with troops; Slovenes, Bosnians and South Europeans, and there was only room to stand. Most of the soldiers were queueing up to make their confessions. The priest was sitting in a chair on the altar steps and they went up one by one and knelt down. Anyone could have heard what they said, if they had cared to listen. They almost all received Holy Communion, and then went on their way to the trenches.

Prince Peter asked me at lunch if I would like to go to Lowicz with him that afternoon. He was going there to see Gutchkoff, the Director of the Red Cross. I was delighted of course. I had heard of Lowicz, where all the people were wearing national costumes. I was enchanted with the dresses of the Lowicz villagers. The women wore massive handwoven petticoats with vertical stripes of red, blue, orange and green, a shawl of the same material, and the handkerchief for the head was a mélange of the gayest colours imaginable. The men wore yellow and black striped trousers like wasps, and their high black boots were laced with magenta bootlaces. It was a delicious feast of colour in a sad world. A very sad world for Lowicz, for the village had been shelled and partly destroyed the day before, and we met a great many people laden with all

67

the possessions they could carry and leaving their homes.

We drove to the castle at Radzivilov, near Lowicz, where Prince Peter had business. They left me in the Great Hall to enjoy the treasures there. The most interesting was a lovely collection of primitive Flemish tapestries. Knights in armour riding proudly over flower-spangled meadows towards fortified castles on the hill, lovely maidens in tall head-dresses waiting to welcome them home. Very civilised. What a pity war is so squalid now.

Two Turkestan soldiers were sentries at the door, and as we were leaving, Prince Peter saw one of them sharpening a long dagger. He asked what he was doing, and the man replied with a grin, "Every night I go out and kill Germans." The men in this regiment had the reputation of being the bravest of all the brave soldiers in the Russian army.

We got back to Skierniewice that night to hear a great commotion and banging of guns, but there were still no wounded. But early next morning, the little horse-drawn carts were coming from the trenches through the trees to our dressing station. It did not look very good, and soon the trickle of wounded became a stream, and we had to look around for more accommodation for them.

The Czar had a private theatre attached to the hunting box, and beside it was a light railway that ran up to the main station at Skierniewice. There was still some scenery about. There had evidently been a pastoral play there last time the theatre was used, and between the nymphs and the shepherdesses, we put down stretchers for our patients.

The foyer was transformed into a magnificent kitchen where Julian, who could do everything, made vast pots of soup, and the women from the Home Farm came along to help. This retreat in the forest was a perfect place for us, and we were a very happy and gay little company. Nick was my very great friend, but all the drivers were delightful boys. I taught them English. Later we had to move again.

It was lucky that we had so few patients left, and some of these were walking cases. It took only about a quarter of an hour to pack them into the lorry and wrap them round with their blankets. As soon as the lorry had gone off with Julian in charge, we turned to the Princess to ask for news of the others.

"They are all safe, thank God, though they were nearly caught. Gutchkoff has ordered them to go to Zyrardow and we are to meet them there. It is dreadful to have to leave all our nice stores here, which we shall have to do, as we have no

Field Hospital

transport, but begin packing and we will take as much as we can."

We hardly had time to pack anything before the car arrived. The driver took us to the main station in Skierniewice. They were making up a train there, and Prince Peter had sent Julian back to help us.

Some of the carriages were full already, and I heard cries of "Sestriza, Sestriza, the train is just going." But this train was going to Warsaw, so we had to wait for another train to Zyrardow.

The Germans were pretty nearly on top of us by that time. We could see the Russian infantry firing steadily from the trenches on either side of the bridge. There was no more shelling, only the staccato tack-tack-tack of machine-guns. Presently that stopped too, and the infantry emerged on our side of the bridge.

They had barely got over when an explosion like the end of the world nearly broke our eardrums. After some of the smoke had drifted away, we could see two arches of the bridge crumble apart and fall into the river.

We all clapped and cheered the soldiers; this would delay the German advance more than a little, we hoped, but it was more than time we were off, and we piled into the train that had just backed into the station. There were five of our company in one compartment - Princess, Basil Petrov, Julian, Marie and myself.

My heart was singing because the drivers were safe, but we were mourning too, because all our equipment was lost. Everything, except some instruments and packages of dressings were left behind in Skierniewice. All our blankets were lost, that perfect-pest-when-travelling, but so-useful-when-we-got-there steriliser, all our stretchers, except a few in the 'ambus', and nearly all the dressings. Retreating again, as usual!

The train crept slowly through the countryside. The sleet froze on the windowpane as it came down and we were nearly frozen too.

Some time in the afternoon, the train stopped. Julian slipped out and came back in a few minutes. This was Zyrardow, and we must get out. The station platform had been shelled away, so we had to collect what equipment we had and step down into a mush of snow and mud at the side of the line.

Although our equipment was not much, we could not possibly carry it and our personal things, so Princess sent Julian to the village to see if he could get a cart, we waiting where we were. It was sleeting hard now, and there was no shelter. The cotton wool cartons and parcels of bandages were getting soaked, and we were frozen right through to our blood and bones. Our empty stomachs kept reminding us that we had not yet had a meal that day.

It was nearly dark when at last we saw Julian coming, leading a horse and cart over the fields. He said he had found a place for all our stuff in a cinema, so we piled everything in and he drove away.

"Red Cross headquarters are here in Zyrardow," Princess said comfortingly. "Gutchkoff will find us a place to sleep, and then we will go and have supper."

It seemed an interminable walk over the fields to the town, but our feet squelched automatically through the liquid pools of half-frozen snow until we reached Red Cross headquarters.

Gutchkoff was away; his secretary was very busy and not at all pleased to see us. No, there was no news of the ambulances of Prince Peter. No, we could not sleep here; there was only one free room and that was reserved for the General who was expected that night. We had better go down to the house where the Red Cross sisters were sleeping, he said; anyone would show us the way. "Excuse me, Excellency," He heard his name called, and walked away. Princess said something in Russian. I could not understand the words, but it sounded gratifyingly rude. Apparently there was no comfort to be got there, so we trudged off to the place where the Red Cross sisters were sleeping.

When we got there, we found it was a tiny cottage with two rooms and a kitchen. There wasn't even any straw; the sisters had put down their leather coats on the wooden floor.

"Go to the factory hospital," they advised. "It is a big place so they must have some beds, and the Directrice will give you supper."

"Where is it?"

"You can't miss it; a big building on the hill at the other end of the village. You must have passed it coming from the station. There is a garden in front. I hope so much you will be all right now and find all you want."

We looked at each other. We were wet through and our heavy clothes added to our exhaustion.

"Courage, mes enfants," said Princess, "it is always darker before dawn."

I tried to make a feeble joke — "And if there is a garden, we can go and eat worms!"

Princess had not heard this saying before, and laughed immoderately. "Come along," she said. "We'll find the garden and eat the worms for supper."

But it wasn't very funny after all. We found the garden all right and the hospital too, but they shooed us away.

"No admittance," the sergeant at the door said, "we have cholera patients here; no one can come in."

Princess called out to a sister who was crossing the courtyard. "Sestriza." She stopped a moment. "What shall we do, Sestriza? There is no room anywhere in Zyrardow, it appears."

"You had better go to the Red Cross place again. They are bound to find something. No one can come in here."

Then she must have seen our fatigue. "Go to the restaurant Warshavsky and get some supper first," she said sympathetically. "You'll get a good meal there. That's where all our sisters eat, and it is just across the road."

The thought of a meal at last gave us strength to get there. It was a dingy hole with filthy tablecloths, but the room was warm and there was a savoury smell of hot meat.

"Can we have a schnitzel?" Princess asked, "and after-wards some tea?"

"Yes, Sestriza," the woman actually said, "in ten min-utes."

Some soldiers by the stove moved up and we toasted our

71

wet legs by the fire. Nobody spoke, we were too exhausted, but our mouths were watering at the thought of the treat to come.

Presently the woman laid a cloth, and brought a dish of schnitzel, cutlets fried a golden brown, and some boiled potatoes. It looked, and smelt marvellous, and I could hardly wait to begin. It was nice in a way, but yet I didn't like it very much; it had a queer taste.

"This meat has a very sweet sort of taste to me, "I said to Marie.

"Yes, " she said placidly, scraping up the last bit of schnitzel, "it's horse."

I suddenly thought of those dead horses at Lodz, with their legs sticking up starkly in the air and I knew I would rather starve. I felt very sick and had to dash out into the dark street.

When I came back, green and sweating, the tea had been served, and the sweet hot drink revived me.

We still had to find a bed for the night, but Princess, who felt like a determined lion after her meal, had an idea. She marched us back to the Red Cross headquarters where the patient Julian was waiting.

"Julian, get three stretchers."

"Excellency."

He produced them from God knows where.

"Put them down in that room they have reserved for the General, and go to bed yourself."

"Excellency."

Julian thoroughly approved of thwarting the General, saluted and went off. If anyone deserved a meal after all he had done, it was Julian.

We took off our sopping shoes and lay down as we were on the stretchers in grateful darkness. It was heaven just to lie still and rest. But there was no heating and the room was terribly cold. We were still very damp, even after the toasting. I kept pulling up one leg and then the other on the narrow stretcher, trying to warm them. The other two were so tired that they were asleep before they lay down.

In the middle of the night, the General for whom the room was reserved, strode in. I heard him say "Chort" (the Devil) when he saw us lying on the floor, and he came round with his torch and examined each of us with great interest. Then he went away and left us in peace. Where he slept, I neither knew nor cared.

We went to the friendly Warshavska restaurant in the morning for some breakfast. The woman had just brought in some tea when Prince Peter came in with Nicky and two of the other drivers.

Princess jumped up and ran forward to greet Prince Peter. His face was a thundercloud, and he did not speak. Nicky came and sat down beside me. He looked desperately tired, but grinned cheerfully. I pushed my glass of tea over to him. "Drink up, Nicky, and do for goodness sake tell us what happened."

"We got cut off," he answered. "I was driving the big 'ambu' and it got stuck in the mud. Alexy and I worked for hours, but we couldn't move it. It was full of wounded, and we had to transfer them to some carts that came along, but I think the poor devils must have been caught; we haven't seen them again. Then we found we had been cut off too, so we took out the little 'ambu' but we didn't dare move until it was dark, so we had to leave the big 'ambu' in the forest. Prince Peter was as mad as a hare, but there was nothing to be done."

"But the new 'ambu', Nick?"

"Yes, the new one; we only had her out twice."

The new ambulance was our greatest treasure. A most beautiful affair fitted up with everything, presented to Prince Peter by the Province of Kazan.

"Oh, Nick, I am so glad you got through – we have all been worrying ourselves stiff. Princess has been very good and not made a fuss, but her face was radiant when you all came in. Where are the others?"

"I don't know, we haven't seen them. But they will probably turn up presently."

"Seychaz, I suppose." "I always teased Nick about saying "Seychaz, Seychaz" all the time. It is supposed to mean 'at once', or directly, but in Russia it mostly means "later on, sometime, never'.

Nick roared with laughter. "Seychaz, seychaz. Exactly." Princess was terribly upset about the ambulance. She took its loss dreadfully to heart, and sat with her head in her hands with the tears dropping down on to her plate. We only had three ambulances left now, including our own.

One evening we were at supper, when we suddenly heard the deep bells of the parish church.

"Mon Dieu, it's Christmas Eve," Marie announced. I could not believe it. I had lost all count of time. Actually, in Russia, Christmas was still ten days away, but here in Catholic Poland, they kept West European dates. In all this turmoil, for the guns rarely ceased, the priests were actually going to celebrate Midnight Mass. I longed to go. Nick, who was a Catholic, said he would go, and Marie, though she belonged to the Orthodox Russian church, said she would like to come with us.

When we got there, though it was an hour before midnight, the church was packed with people from end to end, standing breast to breast for the most part, but some old women were sitting on the altar steps.

It was a very large church, and there must have been more than a thousand of us there, soldiers, townspeople, and a great many refugees from Lowicz, the village I had visited with Prince Peter a few days before. I knew them as they were wearing their traditional peasant costumes. They were looking very much distressed and worn out. They had probably heard the rumour that this front could not hold much longer, and there would be another weary trek for them into the unknown country beyond Poland. Terrified of the brutal Germans behind them, they were almost equally frightened of the Russians. They had a different language, a different religion, a different outlook, and they were apprehensive of what the future held.

When the clock struck midnight, the unaccompanied 'Adeste Fideles' was sung by everybody, and the Mass began.

Presently, a young priest got up into the pulpit and began the sermon. He spoke Polish, of course, and I could understand very little of what he said, but I could watch the effect of his words. When he was speaking of the war, the losses, the sufferings, the deaths, that his people had to undergo, a woman suddenly snatched at her shawl, threw it over her head and began to sob aloud. In a second, the whole congregation began to groan and weep and the church echoed with their cries. The priest stopped for a moment, then held up his hand for silence and began to talk to them in a tender, persuasive voice, pointing to the crucifix that hung above the pulpit. I don't know what he said, but I watched them gradually getting calmer and getting control over themselves as he tried to communicate to them his own joyous security.

Presently, he stopped, and as the people knelt round the altar for the Christmas Feast, the thunder of guns began again, much nearer than before.

The shelling increased all night, and we expected that we should be sent off somewhere, but no orders came.

Princess was better, and she and Prince Peter came over to our Cinema Palace to have Christmas dinner. Julian had not been able to find much, only the inevitable horse, which

I still could not even contemplate taking on my plate. But Princess had a very stale currant cake which had been kept for this occasion, and a little brandy in her flask with which we manufactured weak punch and made cheer with that.

The loss of the ambulance was a terrible hindrance to our work. Instead of being completely mobile, we were dependent on the rare and unpredictable train that was standing in the station which did not even pretend to keep any timetable at all. But this time we were lucky, for the armoured train to Radzivilov still held, and the authorities ordered us to go up the line by the armoured car, which went to the front every second day.

It was waiting for us when we got to the station. Behind the engine was an armoured coach with a few soldiers in it, then two passenger coaches hooked on; lastly some ambulance cars with swinging cots for the wounded.

We started at once and went along very cautiously, stopping every few minutes as no one knew whether Radzivilov was occupied by the Germans or not. It seemed all right, so we went on.

Our order said that the station at Radzivilov had been set up as a Field Hospital but when we got there we found there was no station, just a mass of crumbled ruins. The unit we were relieving had squeezed themselves into the station master's cottage.

The guns were quiet when we arrived, but there had been very severe fighting the last few days. The unit from whom we were taking over had worked without rest for forty-eight hours. They were almost too tired to speak to us.

Wounded men were lying about everywhere, in the little room upstairs, and all over the floor in the large room downstairs which was being used as an operating theatre. The Novgorodski unit was pretty well off for stores, so they gave us some chloroform and bandages, and left us their steriliser until they returned for the next shift. They would be coming up to relieve us in forty-eight hours when the next armoured train came up the line. We helped them pack the wounded into their cots in the 'ambu' coaches and then the engine gave a faint squeak and sidled out of the station in a surreptitious sort

Ambulance train at Radzivilov

Violetta Thurstan: Princess Volkonsky
Russian nurse standing.

Violetta Thurstan, behind her is one of
the sleighs used to carry the wounded

Field Hospital

A ward in a Russian hospital

of way, pretending it wasn't there.

We certainly found ourselves in a particularly awkward place this time. The Germans were trying to get hold of the railway. They had a battery somewhere on our left on the other side of the railway line, and should they throw stuff across at each other, anything that fell short would probably fall on us.

We had begun clearing up when the most awful pandemonium broke out; the battle for the railway had begun again.

A white-faced Russian soldier came running, panting in short gasps, "Mother of God! Oh, Mother of God!" he cried, crossing himself with large sweeps, and began mumbling out a story. I could not understand a word, but the Princess went over to him and tried to calm him. It seemed that a trench had been enfiladed and shelled, and almost all the soldiers in it were killed or wounded. They were bringing fifty wounded men in carts as quickly as they could. It was the most terrible slaughter - men without faces; men with burst bodies and all their entrails hanging out, yet still alive. Another with all the flesh whipped off and the white bones exposed; men unconscious, men groaning, men sweating with pain but not uttering a word. An old, old man with nine wounds. He was a volunteer and this was his first battle. His wife had evidently made loving preparations for him, all his underclothing so clean, so good, his linen shirt beautifully embroidered in red and black. We cut off his grey soldier's tunic. He caught hold of my hand. "Don't cut my shirt, Barina, please don't cut my shirt. My dear wife made it for me."

So I called Julian and Marie to help me, and we eased off the bloody shirt and gave it to him to hold. Poor old Grandad. He died a few minutes after.

Shells were whistling over us all the time. We were so busy we hardly heard them, but they added greatly to the distress of our poor wounded men. Horse-drawn sledges were coming up all the time with more and more wounded. The room downstairs was a shambles of blood, bandages and filthy dressings. The wooden kitchen table was used for operating, the steriliser was hissing in a corner.

Upstairs the patients lay on the floor in the dark; we dared not light a candle. In Skierniewice they had said they would send up another train to evacuate the wounded but it did not come. We had given up all hope of it when at last we heard it purring cautiously in.

It was a terrible job in pitch darkness to get the patients on to stretchers, carrying them down those narrow stairs, and getting them stowed in the train, but at last the little house was cleared, and the train slid away to the base with its piti-ful load.

"Oh Lord," Nicky said, wiping his face, "am I hungry."

"We will eat now," Princess said. "Marie, make some tea. The water in the steriliser is boiling - if Basil has not taken it all!" She smiled at our surgeon who was washing his hands rather lavishly. "Violetta, clear a place for our supper. Nicholas, come with me and unpack the food basket."

There never could be a queerer place for a meal. The only table was the kitchen table Basil had been using for an operating table, now soaked in blood. There were amputated limbs lying about everywhere, dead men in every corner, verminous overcoats that had been cut from patients trailing on the floor, besides the other paraphernalia of a field hospital. I cleared the place up a bit, got some of the paper wrap-pings off the cotton wool and pinned them on to the table, making a clean pale blue tablecloth. Two candles stuck in bottle-necks completed the preparations.

"Ha, ha, Ritz touch I see," Nicky commented. They un-packed the bread and cheese and were putting it on the table when Julian came in and wandered round and round, muttering to himself.

"Julian, what is the matter?" the Princess asked.

"Excellency. I have lost my pail of butter."

"Butter, what butter?"

"I went to a farm and found some butter, Excellency. The people had run away. But I have lost it."

Then he gave a great shout of anger.

"Ah, here is my pail!" He chattered with rage, and began emptying out a nest of dressings reposing on the top of the pail. Someone had seen a pail standing there and, not noticing the precious contents, had thrown swabs on top.

Julian considered awhile, and then fetched a clean knife, removed the swabs, scraped off the top layer of butter, and took some from underneath, put it on a clean plate, and set it down in front of Princess, putting on his 'What a clever fellow I am' face.

"Thank you very much, Julian, but I don't feel very hungry."

Julian assumed his beaten dog act. He didn't care a hang whether any of the rest of us ate it or not.

Basil pushed it down to me. "Violetta?"

"No thank you. I don't think I shall ever eat butter again."

Basil helped himself to a chunk. "Nicky?"

Nicky considered. "Shall I? Shan't I? Shall I?" and finally

took a good portion.

"Nick, how could you? I think you are perfectly disgusting!"

He chuckled, "My dear girl, I don't agree at all. I have to keep strong and fit for my work. I haven't tasted butter for months and months, and this is very good. You will never be any use if you fuss about your food."

"Nick, that is not true. I have never fussed about my food. I simply go without if I can't eat it."

"All English people fuss about their food," Nicky said, pursing up his lips and making a funny drinking face. I was offended, and very much surprised to find myself quarrelling with Nicky.

"Children, don't quarrel," Princess said. "Violetta, don't mind him, he is only teasing you. He used to have an English governess - Miss Gibson, who was very capricious, and we all used to laugh at her."

"Do you think I am capricious, Princess?" I know I said it in an injured voice, though generally I did not mind how much I was teased.

"Not nearly as capricious as I was before the war," Princess said comfortingly. "Before the war I used to lie on the sofa all day and drink brandy."

We all burst out laughing. The thought of Princess, who worked harder than any of us, lying on the sofa and drinking brandy was a good joke.

We could not pursue it further as Julian came in. "There is a soldier at the door, Excellency. He says many more wounded are coming."

"Violetta, fly and boil up the instruments. Nicholas, fetch some more water please."

Nicky gave me a friendly 'Have you forgiven me' wink, but I would not look, and anything I wanted that night I asked Julian to get.

All that night the Germans kept sending up flares, and we were afraid they would discover our little house.

Directly it was light, more and more sledges arrived with half-frozen wounded. The house and the shed behind it were quite full; we must have been two hundred there. We were expecting the train to come up any minute to evacuate them, but it did not come.

There were a lot of dead, and Nick and Julian went out to see if they could dig a grave for them, but the ground was iron hard, and they had to give up.

In the afternoon some staff officers came up, and decided

that it was too dangerous to stay there. We must move two or three kilometres down the line. They said there were a few huts in the new place where some Siberian officers were living, so they would arrange to have an ambulance train sent there. Nothing would be going further up the line, so now we should be the advance post. We could sleep comfortably in one of the coaches, they added solicitously.

We laughed. There wasn't much chance of sleep. We told them we were taking forty-eight hour shifts alternately with our nearest neighbours, the Novgorodski ambulance unit, but they would not relieve us.

The officers were very fussed about our staying where we were, and wanted us to move at once, but obviously we could not leave until our wounded had been removed. They had come up on a truck attached to an engine and one of them volunteered to go and see what had happened to the 'ambu' train. Marie said afterwards that they really thought we were cut off already and that they never expected the train to come at all. But it was waiting further down the line – they had thought it too dangerous to come up in daylight. They had been fired on the day before when going down the line but, luckily, not hit. At dusk, the train crept cautiously in and we packed the wounded in as best we could in the dark.

When they had gone, the officers joined us for tea, and we sat talking until an engine with a truck attached, came to take us to the post further down the line. This interlude made a good break, and we started the night feeling rested.

The relaxed feeling didn't last long though. The second night on duty was awful. One's feet and legs get swollen with the long standing, and it was very hard to keep one's eyes open. I have looked at my watch at seven in the morning, and then after aeons of time looked again, and it was only seven-thirty a.m. Of course the nights, when the wounded were pouring in all the time went by much faster, but there were no wounded this first night in the new place, and we slept like the dead.

Marie was in great feather, as Kolya Andrevitch, one of the Siberian officers in the huts, was the one she had liked so much when he shared our quarters in the cinema at Skier-niewice. We saw a good deal of them now, and they were very good to us. The second time we came up the line after having been relieved for forty-eight hours, we found that they had rigged up a beautiful wooden hut for a kitchen, and got us a boiler from somewhere, so we had the comfort of plenty of hot water. It had now been arranged that the Novgorodski people were to relieve us every twenty-four hours instead of every forty-eight, which made life much more bearable. It was more comfortable for the wounded, too, as we could stow them in the swinging bunks in the train until the armoured 'ambu' train came up to fetch them. The turnover was always at dusk; it was much too dangerous for a daylight journey. Once, though, it did come up early in the morning, bringing Prince Peter up to spend the day with Princess.

The wounded were sent off, there was nothing much to do. Marie and Kolya came along to find me.

"Violetta, would you like to go for a walk? We want to go up the line."

"Supposing a batch of wounded come?"

"Well, there are plenty of people to look after them. Basil is not coming and Kolya thought you would like to come. Do come with us, Violetta."

Of course I said yes; I was longing for a walk. It was a lovely day, blue and frosty and sunny.

We left a message with Julian to tell Princess we had gone for a walk. We did not say where we were going as she would have fussed, and said it was too dangerous.

I walked with Nick and made my peace with him. He was such a darling. I could not imagine how I could have been cross with him. We walked on up the railway line, forests of dark lonely pines on either side of us. It took us about three quarters of an hour to get to our old station.

Nicky and I got there first. Marie and Kolya had fallen behind. It looked inexpressibly dreary, with dirty bandages on the ground, dingy clots of brown blood staining the snow, and far, far worst of all, an amputated leg lay on the platform, half gnawed.

"Nick, let's come away. How hateful and disgusting war is,"

"Well, we see the dirty side of it."

"There isn't anything else to see."

"Well, there is you know," he said in a considering voice, "there's courage and friendship, and other things."

"What other things?"

"Getting away from too much comfort. And us all together. And seeing the funny bits as well as the tragic ones. You don't regret having come, do you?"

"No, Nick, no. I have learnt everything I have ever learnt here. But sometimes it seems so endless, all this suffering and death."

"Do you believe in a future life?" Nicky asked unexpectedly. "I do personally, but lots of people don't."

"Yes, of course I do. But it's this life we have to live just now, and Russia seems so terribly sad."

"Violetta, it isn't always. I promise you it isn't. If you could only see my home. We are friends with our peasants and if you could hear them singing at their work you would know they are happy. You would love the beautiful white nights and the forest and the lakes. We have a country house in Finland you know, and we spend the summer there. I mean, of course, we did, until the war came. You must come and stay with us one day and I'll show you how beautiful it is. We'll bathe in the lake and go riding in the forest. Will you come?"

There rose before my eyes a vision of a time when there was no war, and when Nick and I fished and lay in the sun, and rode through the forest. Nick would be a marvellous play-fellow.

"I should simply love it, Nick, I can't think of anything in the world I should like better. Oh, Nick - what is that?"

But as I spoke, I knew. Suddenly we had come upon a dead soldier lying on his back on the ground, a tall lad about twenty, with flaxen hair and such a beautiful face. His lips were slight-ly parted in a smile, as if he had died in his sleep. He must have fallen off one of the sledges full of dead bodies being brought down from the firing line. What a terribly bad omen, just when we were so happy!

"What shall we do, Nick? We can't leave him here," I said, shuddering at the thought of that awful gnawed limb we had just seen on the platform.

Nick pointed to one of the disused trenches at the side of the railway. "No, we'll bury him. Kolya will help. Hi, Kolya, Kolya," he shouted. Kolya and Marie were a long way behind, but they hurried up when they heard Nick's shout. The boys lifted the body into the trench and filled it up with snow. Marie and I covered it with branches of pine and fashioned a rough cross with twigs. That was all we could do. He had no coat, so we did not know who he was, and could not even let his people know.

He was only one of the millions of nameless dead, but coming at that time, it gave me a presentiment of disaster.

We had to get back, as we knew Princess would be fussing so we returned.

That evening, Marie and Kolya, with Gavrilovitch - one of the engineers from the camp - were sitting in a huddle, their heads together, very excited about something. Marie told me about it when we were going to bed.

"Violetta, would you like to go up to the front?"

82

"Well, we couldn't be much fronter, could we?"

"I know, but I said to Kolya just now how much I would like to go up to the front trenches. You can actually see the German soldiers on the other side of the river you know. Kolya says next time we have a night off, he could fix it with Gavril. Wouldn't you like to go?"

"I should love it, but Marie, wouldn't you rather be alone with Kolya?"

"No, I wouldn't go alone for anything. Kolya is a darling, but he's a very passionate creature. We would both love you to come. Nicky won't come; he says he would rather sleep and he says we are crazy to lose a night's sleep for that. But it would be very thrilling to go."

"Will Princess let us go?"

"Kolya won't tell her very much. He'll just say that Gavril is giving a party and he wants us to come. Let's see - off tonight, on duty tomorrow, off on Thursday. We'll go Thursday night."

"Tell Kolya I'd love to come. I'll try and persuade Nick. It would be marvellous."

Kolya tried all his powers of persuasion, but Princess would not let us go. She was as cunning as a bagful of monkeys and insisted in knowing where the party was to be held. She said Kolya and Marie were quite mad, and Violetta not much better. She would not dream of letting us go. But the next day a most strange thing happened.

Two journalists arrived up the line at our train. One was English, the other American. They brought with them an introduction to Prince Peter, and they had a pass allowing them to stay two days with us if he gave permission. We were very thrilled, especially I, for I had heard so little news from England since I had left Moscow. They were very patient with me, and after I had extracted the last drop of news, they offered me a bundle of newspapers.

I seized them eagerly, but I found I could not read them. I had learnt to live this new, queer life, but it had left me, for the first time in my whole life, without any desire to read. I had brought two books with me, Oxford Book of English Verse and a paper-covered 'Anna Karenina' in French, and carried them through all the vicissitudes of our innumerable treks. Those two books, and a Russian Grammar I had been given at the Smolny, lasted me all the time I was with the unit.

The journalists were mad keen to join our nocturnal expedition and Princess seemed to think their presence cast a cloak of respectability over our wild doings, though I don't think she knew the least of what we were proposing to do.

Gavril grumbled a little that we were too many, but he agreed to supply two carts for us if the front was moderately quiet. Luckily, it was a pretty quiet night and the little gunfire there was died down by sunset.

Nicky looked like a little cross boy when he saw our gay preparations. Pride forbade him to change his mind when the sleighs arrived, and for two pins I would have stayed behind with him, but he was furious when I suggested it. "Oh, for God's sake go off to your trenches, Violetta, and let me sleep in peace. I shall probably have to get out an 'ambu' anyway and bring you all back riddled with bullets. But if that is your idea of fun, get on with it."

We had collected a few presents to take up to the men, a little tea, sugar and some caramels and cigarettes that the journalists had brought up. So, laden with parcels, we packed ourselves into the two carts on runners, each with a stout pony and a soldier as driver. Nicky relented and brought a blanket which he tucked round Marie and me, and whispered into my ear that I must take care of myself. I nearly got out of the cart and said that I had changed my mind, but I did not want to make a fuss, and actually I was longing to go on this exciting trip.

At first we went along the path parallel to the railway line. There was a lovely full moon and with the snow it seemed quite light. Kolya made us take off our Red Cross brassards; he thought they would show up too much light; and then we soon turned up on a right angled path and drove along it until we reached a clearing in the forest where Gavril was waiting for us.

Two sentries with open bayonets were guarding the path and we got out of the carts and left them in their care. It was very dark now that we had got into the forest again. We had to advance along the narrow path in single file. We might not speak, and had to be careful not to let a branch crack.

Presently, we got to a hole between some bushes. Some roughly cut steps led to a big underground chamber lighted by candles; an ikon with a red lamp burning in front of it was in one corner.

Several of Kolya's fellow officers were there and they were surprised and delighted to see our big party. The senior engineer officer fancied that he understood English - "Allo, goodbye, how do you do. Come for supper," he said to Marie and me, shaking hands enthusiastically. They made tea at once, and some vodka was produced for the journalists. These engineers must have had lessons from Julian - they always

84

managed to find something nice to eat. We all clapped when we saw a plate of ham on the table. Ham! I had forgotten there was such a thing. They piled up our plates. "'Ave some more 'am, my darling girls," Grigor said, putting several thick slices on Marie's plate and mine. So, what with laughter and gay chat, not to mention vodka and ham, it was a lovely party.

At last Grigor said it was getting late and we must move if we wanted to go up to the trenches. We left the cigarettes and sweets we had brought, and emerged from our underground shelter. Kolya was looking hungrily at Marie, so I manoeuvred the journalists away to follow Grigor, who was conducting us up to the river where the forward trenches had been dug.

The moon shone on the river below, and we could plainly see the dark gashes where the German trenches were spread out. All was very quiet. We took care not to speak above a whisper, but possibly the Germans noticed some unusual movement for, presently, an attack started and bullets were pattering like hail among the trees over our heads. We got terribly cramped and cold, but we hardly felt it. We were thrilled to be there. After a bit, the firing slackened and they made us go back to the dugout.

A man came in, very excited, showing us the little Ikon he was wearing round his neck. It had saved his life. A spent bullet had passed between the Mother and the Child, and had come to rest in the back of the wooden frame.

They made tea again and then Kolya came in with Marie in an awful fuss, to see if we were all right. He said it was time for us to be getting back, as it would soon be daybreak, and he would not have us there in daybreak for anything. Prince Peter would murder him if he knew.

So we said goodbye, and thanked them for a gorgeous party, and started down to the sentry post. There was a little desultory firing, and after we had got half way, I felt something sting my leg and I fell over a tree stump. The others all said "Hush!" in shocked voices, and I was able to pick myself up and go on. I wasn't sorry to get to the cart though, because I could feel the blood trickling down into my stocking. I didn't say a word; I didn't want to spoil the lovely time we had had and, above all, I didn't want Kolya to be blamed for taking us.

They had got breakfast ready for us when we got back, and we sat down in great spirits, full of our adventure. One of the journalists said, "I was wounded last night."

"Where, where?" we all asked.

"In the face," he said, pointing to a little nick in his chin. "You can all laugh as much as you like, but it means

£100 to me from my paper. I can say I was wounded at the front." They laughed and jeered at him.

I said, "I have a much better one that that in my leg."

They laughed their heads off at that, and insisted on seeing it. It wasn't a very pretty sight; there was a deep graze and profuse blue bruising round it.

"Does it hurt very much?" they asked sympathetically.

"Not a bit," I lied.

Everyone was sensible enough not to make much of it. Nicky put a dressing on, and couldn't resist saying, "I told you so." But I am a pretty healthy person and it soon healed.

I was very much ashamed of the episode that followed our night out. We had a very busy night with an intake of heavily wounded soldiers. The 'ambus' took them all off early in the morning, and Princess sent us off to bed and told us not to hurry in the morning. I woke late, tired and cross. It hardly seemed worthwhile getting up. Then I remembered that there were some dressings to sterilise, and very reluctantly I pulled myself out of bed. I put the cleanest overall I could find over my night things, meaning to go back to bed again as soon as they were done. Marie was still asleep, curled up in her blanket.

Nicky came, whistling as usual, as I was finishing the last swabs, and sat down on a wooden case.

"Put that away, my love, we're going to move."

"Oh no, Nicky, not again. I just can't."

"Can it be that our Violetta is weary of well-doing?"

Something snapped!

"Yes, I am, Nick. I am sick of the war and living like a pig, and always being tired and dirty. And I am very hungry." I hadn't meant to say any of this, but the words came tumbling out. And then the final humiliation, tears began to rain down my face.

"Poor little darling. Don't. I can't bear to see you crying. Cheer up and I'll make you some tea. Give me that kettle."

"It's for the dressings," I protested feebly.

"Dressings be damned! Give me that kettle."

He pushed me down on his wooden case and the tears came trickling down, faster and faster. I could not help it.

He didn't take any notice of me, but went on with his preparations, and presently he brought over two mugs of tea. He held one to my lips with such an air of concern that I had to laugh. He fed me with little sips until it was finished. He then produced a case of rather battered cigarettes, and lighted one for me.

"I wish I could take you away for a week."

I had pulled myself together by then.

"No, I am all right now, Nicky, only terribly ashamed of myself."

"It is our fault. I didn't know how tired you were. I am afraid we must go to Ravka now; it is terribly urgent, I saw the message. But after this one more spell, you must have a little rest, I will arrange it all with Princess," he went on, warming to his theme. "If I could get a week's permission, I could take you to our estate. Our dacha in the country is shut up all the winter; anyway, it would be too late to go there. But my mother is looking after the estate now, and I know she would love to have you."

"It would be just heaven, Nicky. Would it be very wrong of us do you think? Just for a few days."

"I will ask Prince Peter. He will say yes. You have been a heroine and more than deserve a rest. We can't possibly spare you, so just cheer up; nobody but you can cope with that horrible old steriliser. But you must have a respite. Everyone must. I must. I haven't had permission since the war began. Why shouldn't we? I would love to show you my home."

It was something to dream about, and it was wonderful to feel I was really wanted. It was worth all the hardships to know that. But now the ordinary routine claimed us both.

"Violetta, I must go and get the 'ambus' ready; are you sure you are all right now?"

"Absolutely all right. I can't think why I made such a fuss. I'll take some tea up to Princess and Marie and tell them we are going to Ravka."

"Good girl," he said approvingly, and gave me a little flick of a kiss, and was gone.

I put the old battered kettle on again, and got ready for the next move.

All night, as the 'ambus' were bumping along over the pot-holes on our way to Ravka, the wheels were humming to the tune of 'Nuts in May'. "Nicky and I are going away, going away, going away. Nicky and I are going away . . . . "

87

12 RAVKA

Ravka was a small country town, a long high street, two or three little side streets, a church at one end, and a large factory at the other. It was the factory, turned now into a temporary hospital, that we were to take over from our old friends, the Novgorodskis.

We had got used to making an assessment of the situation by now, and directly we got there we could see that our job could only be a temporary one. It was Zyrardow over again. We were almost surrounded by the enemy. The only road not occupied by the Germans was the one we had just come up.

The battle had just begun when we got there. It is no use describing it; it was just the same as any other battle, only worse. More broken men than usual, more wounded horses neighing shrilly, more life, more blood, more shells.

We could see that the Novgorodskis had had more than they could take; they were speechless with exhaustion. We offered to make tea for them, but all they wanted was to get into their 'ambus' and get back to their own quarters. The only thing they could say was, "Thank you, you have come."

We set to work at once. Very badly wounded soldiers were being brought in all the time, and were just plonked down on the floor. I could see that we were in for a bad night. First Nick, and then Julian, was called away to help with the 'ambus'. It was here, at Ravka, that I had the biggest fright I have ever had in my life. If I had not been pretty inured to horrors, I think I should have lost my nerve altogether. As it was, I was pretty shattered until I could pull myself together again.

It was the middle of the night, and we had already almost exhausted our store of bandages. Ravka was the centre in Poland of linen manufacture, and the factory we were working in was one of the biggest linen factories in the country. It suddenly occurred to me that perhaps some bales of linen had been left behind in some of the big cupboards in the lobby; if so, we could make some dressings and bandages. I took a lantern off its hook on the wall and went to the lobby to explore. I opened a cupboard door. No linen; it was full of dead bodies, piled one on another until the cupboard was full! The Novgorodskis must have put them there, not knowing where else to put them and, in their haste to get away, had forgotten to warn us.

I set the lantern down on the floor before I dropped it. It took me a long time before I could bring myself to cross the lobby again. At last I had to rush across the corridor in case anyone came to look for me, and then had to rush across again for the lantern, which I had forgotten. This was to be my pet nightmare for many years to come.

I think the next fortnight was the worst time we ever had. It was worse even than Zyrardow. We were hanging on by our eyelashes, and still there was no let-up in the battle. We were close to the river Ravka which was the pivot of all our defences, so of course General Ivanov had to hang on to it as long as he could.

We had been there about a fortnight when the Princess called Marie and me. "Orders to move tomorrow," she said. I was glad to see that she looked pleased about something, she had been looking desperately worn and sad of late, "and General Ivanov himself is coming here this afternoon. Tidy yourselves up and take a clean overall from the box, both of you. We must try and make a little panache for the General."

She was almost her old gay self when he arrived that afternoon with two or three staff officers. Marie and I thought there must be some good news. She asked the ADC what was cooking and translated his answer to me.

"I don't know if you think it is good news or not, but we've got to evacuate this place for the time being. There are a lot of reinforcements on the way now, and the old man thinks we may be able to stop retreating, and advance a bit for a change. But we'll have to get out of this place first; we can't hold it any longer. We have to straighten the line in front of Warsaw and then, please God, we'll forge ahead."

The General began to make a speech. His front tooth was loose and his words rather indistinct. I couldn't make out a word he said, but I saw Marie looking very hectic, and presently she whispered to me, "We've all three been awarded the St. George, Violetta."

The St. George! The Russian medal given only for service in the field. I didn't believe it; Marie must have made a mistake. But when the General had finished, one of the ADCs handed him three medals with an orange and black ribbon attached, and an official-looking paper, which seemed to be

89

some kind of official announcement. He read it aloud, his front tooth waggling dangerously now, and then he pinned one of the medals on to the Princess's overall, kissing her first on both cheeks. He then beckoned me to come forward, which I did in a dream, convinced that all this was quite untrue, and my cheek was kissed and a medal pinned on to my overall! Marie received the third medal, and a third kiss too.

I was never more surprised in my life. If I had thought about it at all, which I had not, I should have supposed that the Princess might get one, but not Marie and me.

Before he left, we both thanked him, and after talking to the Princess for a few minutes, he and his staff departed, the tooth still intact.

We unpinned ourselves and looked at our precious medals. A portrait of the Czar was on one side, and he looked exactly like our King George; on the reverse side some words were engraved. Marie translated them for me.

"For Valour," she read. "Violetta, I never, never thought of this." She was very moved; there were tears in her eyes. I was still quite incredulous. I felt as big as an ant – I didn't feel I deserved such an honour at all. I was still feeling ashamed of my outburst the day before we left Radzivilov. Princess told us after they had all gone that Ravka was to be evacuated at once and the hospital cleared. There were very few wounded left, and the General gave an order that any new ones must be taken straight to the station. Our Box and Cox, the Novgorodskis unit, was at the station already, and they would look after our patients during their journey to the Military Hospital in Warsaw.

"Now," said Princess smiling and looking very pleased, "the General says we are all to have a little rest. Violetta, your permission has come through, seven days my dear. Marie, you and I are to go back to the Hotel Bristol in Warsaw. We shall rest there for a week and must take care of each other. My husband will join us as soon as he can. Now that the news is a little better, we shall not feel guilty about this little interlude. Basil Petrov is going to his family in Moscow, and the orderlies will take it in turns to look after the 'ambus'. Now I want to congratulate you my dears. I am so proud of you both."

We were certainly very proud of her.

We decided to have a party, and Marie made tea. It was a very queer feeling to have nothing to do. We tried to make it a gala occasion, but we were always jumpy when the 'ambus' were late, and the place seemed very empty without Nicky and

Basil, who were with Prince Peter, and even Julian who had been whisked off to help. We wondered where our 'ambus' were. None of them had come back yet.

Only one more night to be got through, and then Nicky and I would start for his home. I was longing for him to return. I had such exciting news for him - this wonderful permission for us, and about the General's visit, and of course the St. George medal.

Princess would not let us stay up, so we went to bed early, feeling deflated and anxious. Our presentiments grew stronger as the night went on without news, and even if we went to sleep for a few minutes, we woke at every sound. There was a lot of movement outside; there were creaking carts taking wounded to the station, troops retreating from the Ravka salient, gun carriages rumbling by on their way to another position, and in the distance, continuous firing.

In the middle of the night, there was some sort of scuffle at the door and I could hear Princess's voice and a deep man's voice talking. It was not one of our people, and I thought perhaps they did not know that the hospital was closed, and were sending wounded here. Presently, Princess came in to see us. She was shivering, and the candle in her hand was trembling.

"'There is very bad news,' she said. 'One of the officers has just come in to report that several ambulances have been captured, including our own. My husband got away; he and Julian had filled up with some wounded and were already on their way back. They will be here after they have taken the patients to the station.' She stopped, and could not go on for a few minutes. Then her voice steadied. 'I am afraid Nicholas was driving the little ambulance. They think he was shot in the chest and killed instantly. Basil had to take over, but he is not a good driver you know, and was going very slowly in the wrong direction and the officers who eventually got away, think they were captured with four or five other ambulances. General Ivanov has ordered the officer who came here just now to take his staff car and drive us straight back to Warsaw.'"

It was today that my Nicky and I were to start out on the enchanted journey to the shadowed forests and deep flowing rivers of his home in the Ukraine. Nothing mattered any more; I should not even see him to say goodbye. This hateful, hateful war.

Prince Peter got back to Warsaw soon after we did. He and Princess went to their room in the Bristol Hotel. Marie and I sat in ours, too stunned to speak. We were called down presently to lunch, but Marie went alone. For some days I had had a pain in my side, and now it was acute. I was rather glad not to have to struggle any more, and I did not want to see anyone. Presently Princess came along to see me, looking years older. She was very, very kind. Before she left she said, "Violetta, I expect you have guessed. There is nothing left of the unit. No ambulances, no stores, almost no staff. My husband has been talking to the General and he thinks it best if we close down for the present, and perhaps re-form later on as best we can. My husband and I have been discussing what is best for you, my poor child. First you must stay in bed for a few days until you are well again, and then you must go home for a bit and have a good rest. Marie has gone already."

"Can't I come back afterwards, Princess?"

"We should love to have you back with us again, my dear; we have gone through a great deal together, and you have been very good. But I mustn't make a firm promise about anything. Our dear country is in a very sad state. As to the war, we are retreating on all fronts. The winter has been very hard for us. But there is more than that; there is a very great unrest among the troops, great disaffection with the government, great poverty and hunger among the people, and very severe financial difficulties. When you are better, I will get a pass for you to get to England, and you must keep in touch with us. We shall miss you very much. I must get back to my husband - Gutchkoff is here and there will be a conference." She turned to leave.

"One moment, please Princess. Is there any more news?"

"Nothing good I am afraid. The officer who saw our dear Nicholas shot thinks he must have been killed instantly - I know you will grieve, my dear, you were such good friends."

In my heart I knew what Princess said was true. How much longer would Russia be able to hold out? There was terrible poverty and malnutrition in the villages we had been in. The people had seen their horses requisitioned, their fields trampled, their houses shelled. There was no longer any money; there were notes now, even for a farthing. They had no hope of winning the war now. The soldiers, so patient and loyal in the beginning were discontented, disillusioned, angry - how much longer? Was Russia really finished? I wondered if she would rise again some day.

Ten days later, I was on the train to Petrograd. Katrina, one of the Novgorodski unit who had so often relieved us, was on the Warsaw platform, and told me she was also going to Petrograd.

"My grandfather has died," she said, and I am going back for the funeral; we must travel together."

After three days of hard travelling, we arrived at the Petrograd station, and she begged me to come home with her. I did not want to very much, I would rather be alone, but I could not refuse. I had planned to go to the British Embassy and see Lady Georgina and tell her that I was on my way home, but Katrina was in a very nervous state, and I did not feel I should desert her, so we went to the apartment where her grandfather lived. There was no one in the flat; the dead grandfather was lying on his bed in the bigger bedroom of the two. Katrina was to sleep in the small dining-room adjoining. She made up a bed for me in the sitting-room.

It was very late and we went straight to bed. I could not sleep. I could only think of the dead grandfather next door. After lying awake for hours, I could not bear any more. I had an irresistible impulse to fly from the house. I did not want to wake Katrina, so I dressed in the dark, left my suitcase by the bed, and slipped out of the flat. I remembered the way to the dark and dismal Finland station where I had first arrived aeons before, and waited several hours until the train for Sweden arrived at last.